SIEGE OF THE UNFINISHED KEEP

Epic of Hornblood Castle #1

Eric Kercher

Paper and Sword, LLC

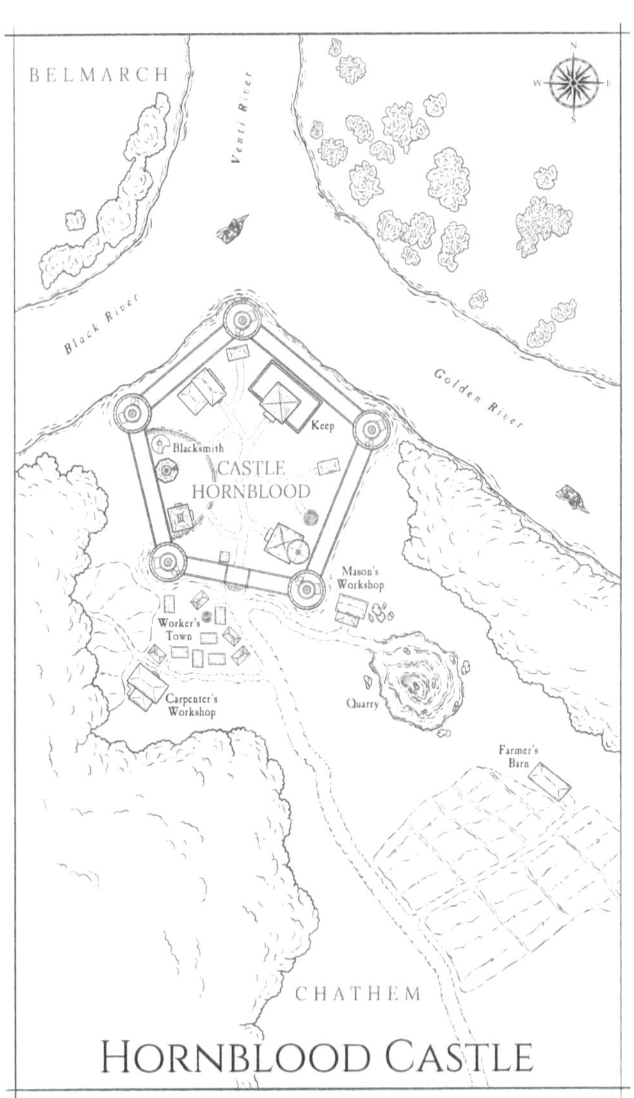

HORNBLOOD CASTLE

For Mark and the lessons he taught, the duty he carried, and the love he showed.

FROM THE AUTHOR

There are days when we all need an escape from a terrible job, a terrible day, or a terrible life.

Join my newsletter and get an escape from the real world, stories, and lore designed to entertain and delight.

You'll also get *Stories from the Deep*, an exclusive, unpublished anthology chock full of extra epilogues, short stories, and lore from the Patmos Sea Fantasy Adventure Series.

Join now at erickercher.com.

Enjoy the book.

-Eric Kercher

1

The Tower

Sun poured in the opening, the rock walls rising like sentinels to either side. Sam examined the openings, barely big enough for the beam, and wondered how he was going to do this.

"Can we take out a few stone?" he asked.

"Not on yer life," Bill said. He picked up another stone, wiped his nose with the back of his sleeve, and buttered it with mortar. The haze of the morning had burned off hours ago, but the smell of moisture from the river hung in the air like a blanket. Somewhere off in the distance, a bird called, loud enough to be heard over the sound of masons' hammers and breaking rock.

Thoughts turned over in his head, options to cut it down to size. Aggravation was at the back of his mind, but it was too late to do anything about it now.

The rest of the castle building was hard at work, the early morning breakfast long over. The sun hung halfway up the sky, closer to the noon meal than morning, and soon it would turn and make its descent to the west.

"What are we going to do?" Beside him, Trent wrung his hands. The boy was too full of worry by two hands, but Sam didn't get to choose who his apprentice would be.

Sam looked down, the beam that was to take the main position on the ground beside the wall, and walked around the perimeter of the tower.

The beam was long enough to cover the span, but would need to be cut to size and ends shaped to fit into the strange sized opening that the masons had left him. Sometimes he wondered if Bill did it on purpose, or if it was sloppy work. He opted for the ladder but couldn't rule out the former.

The problem was the cross members. How was he going to get them in? "Take the twine, we'll measure the opening and get to work."

Trent took the other side across the gap, twelve feet up to the floor below. That floor had been easier, they were able to incorporate the big wooden beams into the walls of the keep, but now the circles of the tower left the walls behind and rose above them, leaving him little room to work with.

He tied off the other end, checking both corners, and then knelt back to wait as Trent transcribed the opening size onto an offcut of wood.

When he was done, they left the top of the tower, descending to the dusty ground below. Sam puzzled over the problem while they walked.

They cut the beam to length, carved the end to size, and then had it attached to the crane before the supper meal, with a brief stop for lunch beneath the shade of the walls.

Sam stood up, wiped the sweat off his brow, and peered at the cloudless blue sky. "We'll get this up tomorrow."

"Mortise and tenon?" Trent asked.

"Possible. Let's go back and see how the other beams are coming." He picked up his tool bag, leaving the beam tied up, and together they started for the workshop.

"Oy," Bill called down. "Are you leaving?"

"Yes," Sam cupped his hands and called back.

"I need the crane. Untie your beam."

Suppressing a note of irritation, Sam sent Trent back to take care of it, promising to meet him at the workshop. *He could have told me earlier.*

No doubt Bill was going to blame him for a work stoppage again, and he would hear about it in the morning. Sam tried to relax, stretching his shoulders and arms from the long day hauling the beam around.

The smell of wood shavings and dust entering the workshop made him feel better. Ned stopped his dressing of a beam and nodded. "All goes well?"

"As well as could be."

"Ah, Bill giving you more trouble?"

"Nothing I can't handle." Sam hung his tools on the peg near the workshop opening. It creaked ominously, and he watched it. "Must do something about that..."

Kerien was hard at work planing the beams they needed, his plane scraping across the surface. A ribbon of wood shaving curled up from the opening, before he took it out and tossed it to join the growing pile of them at his feet.

Sam examined the surface, feeling across the grain. It was smooth, a good sign Kerien had sharpened his plane. "Good work. Check for high spots here." He pointed to a rise on the top. "Needs to be smooth for the floorboards."

Kerien looked both relieved and annoyed, the emotions flashing across his face. "Will do," he mumbled. Sam patting him on the shoulder and joined Ned at the water pail, taking a deep draught after him. The old man's eyebrows were long and bushy, and he peered out at him from under them.

"Something's bothering you."

Sam shook his head, taking another drink. The water was warm from being out all day, but still refreshing. His skin had run out after lunch, but he didn't have time to get more. "Just thinking about this connection. We can't just do it like the others, the span is too large."

"What about smaller spans?"

"Will that work?"

"It should." Ned, as excited as Sam had ever seen him, talked him through his idea using bits of stick and offcuts. For not the first time Sam wondered why Ned hadn't been chosen to lead the carpenters over him. He had far more experience, and had worked in fortifications before.

Trent walked in, proceeded to his station to start his next task, and Sam glanced up at him.

His brow was furrowed, and he avoided eye contact with Sam. Something happened.

"How is he?" Ned asked quietly.

"Coming along." It was true, despite his age, the boy was a hard worker, if not the most efficient. Sam could wish for seasoned carpenters all he wanted, but he worked with what he got.

"They denied the request, didn't they?" Ned watched him with clear, brown eyes that hid a mountain of wisdom.

"No volunteers."

Ned snorted. "They'll have to raise pay if they want volunteers." His bushy eyebrows wriggled. "I'll never see that in my life."

"Never say never." They went back to the problem, and Sam wished he had Louis back. He would know what to do, or know faster.

"You haven't put the beam up yet, have you?" Ned asked.

A grip of realization took Sam. They were about to put it up, three stories into the air. "No, we had to take it off for Bill to use the crane."

"Well, that was a help, and he didn't even know it." Ned chuckled, the wrinkles at the corner of his eyes deepening. "Give me a few minutes to think on this."

Sam nodded and moved off, talking to each carpenter in turn. Kerien had fixed one of the high spots, but had torn the grain in his haste. The pile of lumber in the yard caught his eye as he spoke.

Sam shook his head as he moved on. It was getting low. He would have to send out another team to the forest for more raw lumber soon. They were going through what they had on store fast.

Trent was finishing up the beam preparations, using a square to even out the sides. He was slow, only one side was done, and Sam checked his work.

There were gaps in the square along most of the beam, but a few sections were so far out he grimaced. "Here and here," he said, pointing them out. Trent looked crestfallen. "You're improving, boy, don't give up now." He handed the square back.

The smell of dinner was wafting in the opening, brought in with the evening wind. It came from the southwest, the prevailing wind direction. He hurried on to Archie and Stu, journeymen that were almost ready for full carpentership. Bob was working on a door frame, finishing up preparing the stock, and was coming along nicely. He would work on the door next, if they had enough oak to finish it.

They had finished their tasks for the day. "What should we do tomorrow?" Bob asked, hanging up his apron. The dinner bell would be ringing soon. They both looked toward the door. That was a good question. After this section of the tower, they would need flooring. No one had started it yet.

"Take down a few more trees tomorrow. Straight oak is preferable, but anything straight will do."

They nodded. "Go ahead."

Without hesitation they were gone, out of the workshop and straight to the food. The bell rang out seconds later, and the rest of the workshop put up their tools.

Sam stayed behind, thinking about what was left and what was upcoming. The sun was casting its colors into the sky, and he leaned on the workshop porch to watch it.

Castle Hornblood stood imposing before it, a skeleton of what it would be. The great walls of limestone glittered gray in the sunset. It was made of stout, hefty stone.

That reminded him. The quarry asked for another crane. Who he was going to get to do that he wasn't sure, but they had one about to fail. It was there since the beginning and had seen plenty of use.

A few more loads and it might snap in half. Sam sighed, hung up his apron, and joined the others at dinner.

The Square was abuzz with conversation and alive with light. A cheerful fire burned in the center, with the remains of a deer still turning on the spit and sizzling as it dropped fat. The smell drifted over everything and mingled with fresh bread. Sam didn't even mind the undercurrent of unwashed bodies it smelled so good.

He got in line for the food, which had dwindled since he was so late. he was behind a pair of masons talking about the woes they had to deal with.

He made his greetings and listened to the life around them. There was a touch of sadness in his gladness. Families now joined the workers, contributing all the chaos and joy that accompanied them.

Children played and ran in between the legs of their parents in great packs. The women added a touch of comfort in the hard wilderness they occupied, and food was by far his favorite contribution.

"Evening Sam," Twilight said, winking at him. "Some of everything?"

"Please." He took the wooden plate, holding it out over the thick stew that she spooned onto it. A chunk of bread, fresh from the morning, added a garnish besides a slice of venison that still steamed. "Much obliged. You always have a way with food that I appreciate."

"On, get along now," she said, waving a hand at him and blushing, but she looked pleased. He knuckled his brow and went to join Ned at a table, along with a few of the other carpenters.

The masons shot him a look as they took their plates, one mumbling something under his breath to the others. Sam didn't fail to notice.

It troubled him, just another thing to add to the pile of unresolved problems. How could he work with Bill?

The food was good, and hot too, almost too hot. It burned his tongue, so he let it cool. The weak ale that came with the meal helped with the sting, but couldn't remove it.

He let his stomach grumble as his food cooled, making small talk with the others.

"Sam, there you are." The voice boomed behind him, and he winced.

"Overseer Clayton," he said, rising. "Evening to you."

"What is the meaning of holding up the work at the southeast tower? I was told you took up the crane almost all evening." The Overseer brought all eyes to him, silencing the crowd.

Sam cleared his throat. The tips of his ears burned hot, and he fought the anger that bubbled up inside. He thought he would at least have until the morning. "We were unaware that the — "

"Enough of your excuses. How many times do I have to tell you how critical this castle is?" Whispers in the crowd brought his attention, and Clayton rounded on them, shaking a large fist in their direction. "And don't think all of you are free of this, either. I've seen how you sulk and shirk your work. Need I remind you how close we are to Belmarch?"

The Square was silent, except for the crackling of fire and hisses of burning fat. Someone nudged the spit worker and they resumed rotating it, the creaking joining in.

"You'll see me in the morning," Clayton said, turning his haggard eyes back to Sam. "And leave your excuses when you do."

2

OVERSEEN

The night didn't go well. Sam's food tasted like ash in his mouth, but he dutifully swallowed it. He didn't know when they'd have meat again, but doubted it would be soon.

The others gave him a wide berth, letting him alone. He caught a couple glances from the masons, giddy with a hidden mockery, but they didn't say anything outright.

The time came for him to retire, and he bid the others good night. Instead of going back to his hut he went out to the edge of the small town that had been erected and stood at the edge of the farms.

Small puffs of wind tousled the sprigs of greenery and rattled the trees. The wind was dying down for the night, like it usually did, and the sky was half covered in clouds. The stars twinkled above him with a sliver of moon carved out in the eastern sky.

This wasn't the kind of life he was hoping for. He squeezed his eyes shut, imagining what it would be like to be someone else. If Fannon was here...

The chill of the night wore through his clothing, and Sam retired his thoughts and turned back to the simple hut he called home.

It wasn't much, but with his station he was afforded privacy. A bed, a table, and some belongings in a trunk made the majority of the furnishings, with a chair he made himself.

It wasn't the prettiest thing to look at, but it held him up well on three legs. He sunk into it, leaning back against the stiff frame.

What was he supposed to tell him? That he didn't know what he was doing? That he should find someone else to lead the carpenters?

Ned wouldn't do it, and none of the others were even masters. They needed more craftsman here, if the building was going to work, but with the completion of the outer wall there didn't seem to be much desire to finish it.

Day after day they looked for barges and ships coming up river loaded with more recruits to raise the castle. Day after day they were disappointed.

Even the masons were tired, despite the large numbers, and Sam wondered if this wasn't done out of necessity instead of spite.

That wasn't something he thought of before, but he realized it might be the case.

The night was waning, and his body called for rest. Sam yawned and shed his outer garments. After he slipped into bed he decided to go to Bill in the morning and see if there was anything he could do.

This castle wasn't going to build itself.

The roosters woke him. He was grateful to be awake, the strange dreams of a nightmare haunting him.

He had been back in full armor, weighed down and trapped in quicksand, all his family just out of reach. They called to him with gaunt faces and outstretched hands of the palest white, beckoning him on.

He didn't want to go there, wherever it was, and tried to escape, but the sand pulled him closer, trapping his legs and arms and sucking at his neck.

He still felt the coarse grains at the base of his chin and rubbed it. Nothing there.

It was all a dream, too real to be anything else.

Sunlight poured in the slat covered window, another perk of his position. He dressed and pushed open the door to the early morning world.

Others were already out, the farmers and wives in the field, tending to the hardest work before the heat of the day. Gruel was kept warm over the fire and he took a bowl.

It wasn't good, but it filled his belly, and kept him in good enough cheer to keep him alive.

Although, he would have to face the Overseer soon. The man slept in late, so he had some time.

He was the first in the workshop and kindled the remains of the fire with offcuts and shavings to a pleasant size. It was almost time to re-oil all the handles, but he had none to speak of.

He might, if he still had a position after this meeting, be able to beg some from the Overseer. They did still get some shipments from the south, and oil might be available.

But all of this, he knew, was just a distraction. He would have to face the Overseer on his own.

The others were coming in, and he greeted them. They looked at him and slipped by, and he tried to soften his expression, but they got to work and kept their heads down. Little conversation flowed. The sounds of work abounded as the sun rose. He glanced outside and knew any longer would meet nothing but anger.

"I'm off, everyone keep working while I'm gone." He expected something, but was greeted with silence. Even Ned didn't look up.

So Sam turned and left, walking the path up to the castle keep and toward the entrance.

Sunlight still streamed in from above, shining on the first floor, and sneaked its way into cracks down to the bottom level. There were no doors on the main entrance hall, another thing Sam and his crew were supposed to do, so he walked in the large stone arch and down the hall to the first door on the left.

He was inside, talking to someone else, as Sam paused just outside to take a deep breath. The air was dusty and filled with the droppings of the masons far above.

Sam rapped on the thick wooden door, remembering that he helped make it. Vaguely, he sensed a moment of pride before the voice came through it. "Enter."

He didn't sound pleased, although a lot of the bite that had been in the Overseer's voice was gone. Either by a good night's sleep or the dulling of time, Sam hoped it might turn out better than he expected.

Overseer Rhys was inside, with a young man of about twenty. The thick black hair gave it away, he was a Hornblood.

"Come in," the Overseer said, his eyes clouded. He sat behind a paper-strewn desk covered in the plans of the castle. It was oversized to hold them all, and Sam was sure his desire was for a far more elegant desk, for the Overseer was a sophisticated man. Why he ended up here in charge of the production of the building was still a mystery to him.

Silence reigned, and Sam took his spot in front of the desk dutifully, staring straight ahead.

The wood of the Overseer's chair squeaked as he leaned forward and steepled his hands. "Is there a reason why you keep interfering with the mason's work?"

"Not trying to interfere, sir." The room smelled of tobacco and sweat, the trace lingering of a pipe still around.

"Then why do they keep coming to me, saying you're putting them behind?" His voice was calm, for now. Sam wondered if it wasn't due to the Hornblood onlooker.

"I imagine we keep them from advancing from time to time. I'm trying to get everything done."

"Trying." the Overseer scoffed. "I've given you everything you need, and yet you still make excuses." He slammed a fist down on the table, making it jump. Sam kept his eyes fixed on a point above him where an interesting section of stone met. "If it weren't for the deadline, I'd have you removed and sent upriver to the nearest drop off point."

Sam bit his tongue. Better to get it over and done with than worry the man any longer. "Yes, sir."

"I want you to think carefully about what needs to be done and work together, in harmony, with everyone else. Is that clear?"

"Yes, sir."

"I said, is that clear?" Sam met his eyes, fiery behind the puffy cheeks.

"It is clear, sir. Is there any word on recruits?" Sam had to press this. "We could use a few more--"

"Enough!" the Overseer thundered, rising from his chair and toppling it backward. "You'll get what you get," he calmed himself, straightening his shirt and slicking back his black hair. "Dismissed."

Sam dropped his head a small, but respectful, amount and left.

He breathed a sigh of relief as he shut the door. It could have been worse, and it could have gone better. He suspected the Overseer was holding back, but whatever the case may be he still had a place here.

Now, he just had to finish the work. Behind him he heard voices, but couldn't make out what they were saying through the door. He resisted the urge to listen and left, back out the wide open arch to the outside and down the path.

The sun was up in the sky now, burned off the last wisps of morning. Sam whistled in the bright morning air, some of the weight off his shoulders.

Once again, he would live to fight another day.

He glanced up at the tower. Bill watched him with a glower, but Sam just waved and walked on. *No need to upset him now.*

As he walked along the dusty path to the workshop he wondered who the newcomer was. The Hornbloods were set to take residence in the castle, it was their land, after all, but hadn't been seen before now. It couldn't be the Duke, not with him being so young, and he suspected it might be a son or a distant cousin. Maybe a nephew to come see how things were going.

Sam brightened at the idea that they might have another report that would put their situation to light to higher ups. It might be the thing they need, to finally get more workers and more support.

And, if truth be told, more soldiers.

He glanced over, the Ventie River running clear right behind the forest. A few more stones on the tower and they would be above the trees, and with a good view to the other side.

To the Belmarch side.

Which meant they could be seen in turn. He wondered what it was like there, as much as the stories told of death and destruction, he knew it couldn't be that bad.

Although the thirst for war and blood seemed to be real, considering the stories that were told. Invasion, raids, attacks. They had carried them out in spades.

Which, he supposed, is why the castle was being built. Stationed at the headwaters of the Streaming Split, the division of the Venti River into the Golden River on the east and the Black River on the west, the castle allowed for a defensive position at the best river crossing from Belmarch in to Chathem.

It would be where he would have chosen a defensive position, too. Sam shook his head. That life was behind him now, long gone. He was a carpenter, a worker of wood.

He longed for the feel of it, warm and smooth or roughed from a new split, and the smell of it. Fresh, clean, newly felled, or dried and sawn, wood dust brought him to simpler times, a time of peace.

And, hopefully, a time of prosperity. As much as he disliked being Master Carpenter, the pay was better than as a worker alone.

A child waved to him, Netty's girl, he thought, and he waved pack. She turned back to her playmates, chasing after one another in the dust.

A low rumble in the distance brought his attention to the sky. Lightning lanced through a thunder head far off. It might be coming this way.

Sam quickened his step and soon found himself back at the workshop. Anxious eyes looked to him, and he smiled. "I'm still here, for the time being."

"We hoped you would be," Ned said, hand on a plane.

"What did he say?" Archie asked.

"Nothing that bears repeating to your ears. Hush now and get back to work. We'll have a difficult time if we don't get that beam up before it rains." Sam looked around. "Where's Trent?"

"Up at the castle. He brought your tools and said he was going to start without you." Sure enough, his tool hook was empty.

Sam checked to make sure everyone had enough work for the next few days and left. A part of him admired the initiative Trent showed. Another part of him wondered what he would mess up.

But by the time he got to the tower, Trent hadn't progressed much past marking up the end of the beam.

Sam stopped, collecting his breath, and examined his work. Everything was laid out as they expected, with two sides marked. He nodded, and Trent took out his saw and started working, cutting away the meat of the wood back to just outside his line.

Sam turned his attention to the middle. After his discussion with Ned, he thought he knew what he was going to do.

"You're in our way," a familiar voice said. Sam turned. Bill, and three of his masons, stood with arms crossed and hammers ready, scowling at them.

3

BEAMWORK

"Good morning to you too." Sam eyed them. Their pupils were dilated and, judging from the smell wafting in his direction, they had found their way into the ale earlier.

"I didn't say it was a good morning," Bill said, deepening his scowl.

"What is it you would like?"

"For you and that sod to stop getting in our way." Bill pointed his hammer at Trent. Sam stepped in between them, causing the other masons to spread out and enter a fighting stance.

Sam held up his hands. "We don't want any trouble."

"You've got it," one of the masons said, a slight slur to his speech.

"Hold on," Bill said. He smiled. "We want to work, that's all. Like he said, no trouble."

"Can we discuss this in a more...private setting?" Sam kept his voice low, hoping that Bill was the only one who had heard.

He scoffed. "I think not. Why don't we help them boys?"

The masons advanced, and Sam stepped back. He pushed Trent away, the boy quivered, and they stepped out of the way.

Bill watched him as they picked up the beam and chucked it down the hill. It tumbled, striking the rocks on the way down, before it finally rested at the base of the wall.

"There. Now we can get to work." Bill walked up to Sam. "Next time you get in our way, we won't be so accommodating."

"We aren't enemies," Sam said. Bill showed him his teeth.

"Just stay out of our way." Bill walked past, shouldering him out of the way. Sam stepped aside, letting him go.

"Why didn't you do anything?" Trent's face was flushed, and his eyes were watery. Sam put a hand on his shoulder.

"Come on," he said. He felt Trent's eyes boring into his back, assuming he was a coward. He felt a touch of it, but there wasn't anything he could do about it. He was here to build, not to destroy. "There's a way to break anything, given the right leverage. It's harder to make."

They trudged downhill to the beam. Sam examined it, running his hands along the dents and scratches it had picked up along the way. The ends were blunted, but they were going to be cut anyway. Miraculously, it was still intact and sound enough to put up.

"Help me with this side," Sam said, stooping down to pick up one end. He gave a count and they lifted it, turning it one revolution, and pulled it up the hill. It had taken the four masons to pick it up, but the two of them struggled.

They stopped to take rests, setting back on the ground every few yards. Sam felt it in his back at the top, the burning of his muscles and arms.

It had taken the cart to get it up here, and at least a half an hour to return it by hand. Trent wouldn't speak to him, and avoided his gaze. Still, Sam went over the cutting with him, instructing him and watching him when he needed to.

He wasn't going to abandon his development over a little tussle.

While Trent cut the ends, he worked on the mortise at the middle. He laid out his sizing and scored along the edges of the hole, about a quarter of the way from the edge of the beam, and then got to work using a chisel to hollow it out.

It was still sharp from when he had sharpened it this morning and made quick work, deepening the hole and creating a pile of chips to each side. He was halfway through when Trent needed to turn the beam and performed the same operation on the other side, but a little smaller to account for mis-measurement.

Slices of wood fell away as he cut. The chisel gleamed in the light of the morning, reflecting the sun and scattering it into tiny shards of light.

Sam leaned down and blew into the hole. Chips and shavings flew out, then drifted down around the opening and ground. He brushed them off, enjoying the smell of the oak as he cut it.

He let himself sink into his work, letting the confrontation slip away. The music of the castle under construction lulled him. Slamming rock, hammer blows, the ring of metal. A rope creaked as the crane hauled another load of rock to the top.

Inch by inch, stone by stone, beam by beam, the castle was coming together. When Sam finished his mortise he stood up and stretched his back, admiring the work they had put in so far.

He hadn't been here for the initial laying of the walls and outlays, but now they towered above him. The keep was well under way, the next priority, before they build the rest of the outbuildings and support structures other than the blacksmith.

Their area was finished, tucked up against the wall. Smoke poured out of the chimney, a fire blazing in the furnace.

He wiped his sweaty brow, glad he didn't have to be there on a hot day like today. The sun wasn't at the peak of its journey and already his clothes were soaked with sweat.

"Done with this side, too." Trent stood over his work, shuffling his feet from side to side. He still wouldn't look him in the eye.

Sam passed his hand over the work, comparing it to the form they had used. He pointed out a few more areas to knock down.

"First, let's move these cross members over. Might as well cut it on the ground."

He had another beam ready, a few yards away down the slope. They went and pulled it from its resting place, setting it up on an offcut to suspend it off the ground.

Sam took one end of the saw and Trent took the other. They started it roughly in the middle, rasps that hit a steady rhythm as each man pulled the saw back and forth.

The teeth cleared out packs of sawdust that puffed out the sides and sprinkled onto the grass. The lunch bell rang just as they finished, the beam falling away into two on either side.

Sam dusted off his hands and left the beam where it lay. "Come on, we'll eat and come finish this after."

After putting away the tools, safe from prying eyes and hands, they walked down the road with the stream of other workers back to the Square.

Up ahead, the movement around the fire seemed more pronounced. When they got there the Square was abuzz with activity and conversation.

"What's going on?" Trent asked, eyes wide, as they reached the table the other carpenters had claimed.

"New lord," Ned said, ripping off a hunk of bread and dumping it into his stew. "Brought a world of trouble, it seems."

"How so?" Sam asked. He waved off a fly buzzing around his head. The soup smelled good. Leftover venison, no doubt, or the bones. He suppressed his hunger to listen to the stories around him.

"Young Hornblood, distant cousin or something like that. Says the Belmarch have rumblings of war and raiding parties."

"I heard they came over the river a few miles down and killed an entire village. Didn't even take them as hostages, just burned the place down. They said the bodies were left all charred and blackened," Archie said. Trent's eyes widened even more.

"Hush now, none of those rumors," Sam said.

"It isn't rumor. I heard the same thing, that the peace isn't holding anymore and they'll be across." Kerien held up a defiant chin.

"These Belmarch aren't that bad. It must be bad blood making tall tales." Sam stood to get in line.

Ned shook his head. "I'm afraid not. I've lived up north my whole life and what they say about the Belmarch is true. A bloodthirsty, horrible people that love fighting amongst themselves more than they do fighting others." He gummed a hunk of bread, some soup dribbling down his chin. "That's the only thing that's kept them from invaded and conquering us so far."

Sam was sobered. He had heard tales about them raiding and pillaging, but had assumed they were exaggerated before. Ned wasn't prone to tall tales, and even less to lying.

"They aren't going to get us, are they?" Trent asked. His hands gripped the bench, knuckles white.

"We've got a wall to keep them out," Sam said before any-one else could open their mouths. "You'd best remember that we have a job to do and can't be distracted from it. Trent, come get your supper."

The line had died down, only two in front of them. The smell of the soup was stronger here, mixed with the smoke of the fire. Sally spooned his portion out with a few kind words, which he returned, and he went back to join them.

The other groups of men and women cast furtive glances around and spoke in whispered tones. Sam met their gaze where they could, seeing something of fear inside.

There might be something more to these tales than he had thought.

Kerien was in the middle of one when they returned, capturing all the attention of the others. Sam picked it up midway through the story. "They took the women first. Did unspeakable acts to them. The men were forced to watch. They begged them to stop, but they only laughed.

"They slaughtered the animals next, forced the women to cook them, and then when they were done with their feast and their...acts." He paused, and the others leaned in. Sam took a spoonful of the soup and blew off the steam. "They killed the men and dumped their bodies into the river. They floated down, discovered by the towns below. A day later, they saw the women. Then the children."

"Horrible," Archie said, face contorted in pain.

"That's not the worst of it. They ate the hearts of the chil-dren." The others recoiled.

"Why would they do that?" Trent asked, as white as a sheet.

"Some say they're possessed by demons. Other say it is to grow more powerful."

"Whatever the reason, keep them as far away on that side as possible." Archie shuddered and Trent clutched at his flagon.

"The word is the Belmarch are on the warpath again. That's why they've sent a Hornblood here. They say there's a warlord withing Belmarch that is unifying them."

"A unified Belmarch? God forbid," Bill said.

"We should expect them to attack soon."

"On what authority do you speak?" Sam asked, setting down his spoon.

Kerien paled a little, then dropped his gaze to his soup. "Things I've heard around," he mumbled.

"Rumors then?" Sam arched an eyebrow. "Kerien, I'm disappointed in you."

"We all know they would do it if they could. Why do you think we've finished the walls first?"

"No sense in scaring anyone about it."

"You've right to be afraid of them," Ned said. "They're monsters walking in the form of men." It cooled his head to hear Ned say it.

"Either way, we won't speed up the work thinking on it any."

"That's just it, we're going to be trained to fight." Sam's head snapped to Kerien.

"What?" Bill asked, mouth gaping.

"That's one of the reasons the Hornblood is here. He's brought with him his head guard to train us in combat. No spare swords around, apparently."

This rumor, if true, was the worst. Sam's mind wandered back to darker days. Days he had tried to escape from as much as possible.

Could they be catching up to him?

He steadied his hand on his bowl and took a spoonful into his mouth. He held it there, feeling the chunks of potato and the wetness of the stock, then swallowed.

It went down like a lump of stone and settled in his stomach next to the feeling that had developed.

Fighting was someone else's business. There was no way he was going to get caught up in it.

The others talked about the developments, gossiping about the Hornblood, but Sam let it all wash over him. He didn't even scold them like he would have, his mind was too preoccupied.

Before he knew it, the work bell was ringing again. The workers got up at once, and in a wave went to the castle.

Sam was swept up with them, the others going back to the workshop and Trent and he up the hill with the rest.

His feet carried him without thinking. They were back at the beam already, and Trent was at his side.

"Master Freeman?"

"Yes?" Sam looked down at him.

"Should we get back to work?"

"Oh, yes." he wondered how long he had been standing there without moving. A minute? Or longer? "Take that side, we need to cut these to fit."

As he worked to carve off the tenon, checking his cuts as they went, Sam's mind was on a different time.

And a different place.

4

THE THUNDER THAT WAITS

The sky darkened in the south, a mass of clouds gathering on the horizon. Sam felt the rain before it hit and smelled it on the wind. He frowned and watched the sky, waiting for it to open and pour out its water to the earth.

They didn't get as far as he liked, but leaving it out in the open would have spoiled the timber. So, begrudgingly, he called a halt to the work and they pulled it under a nearby lean-to just in time for a great mass of water from the sky.

It bounced off the rocks and splashed up from the ground to soak his pants. The courtyard was mud in an instant, a chaos of carts and horses and men running to and fro to try and get out of the rain.

"Why don't you tell them to go away and leave us alone?" Trent was hunched in the corner of the lean-to while Sam looked out into the rain. He was hoping it would blow over, but there was too much water for that to be a possibility. This would wear itself out, but not before they needed to get back to the workshop.

The question, however, disturbed him from his thoughts of the past. "It will be better to find a way to work with the masons. We won't be finding ourselves rid of them anytime soon."

"But what they did, what they do..." he trailed off.

"These men aren't our enemies, Trent."

"They certainly aren't our friends."

Sam had to let out a laugh. How naïve. Had he ever been that foolish, that unseeing? "They have a job to do, and they're as low on manpower as we are. But, not only do they have less men than they should, they have far more work."

He spread his arms around him. "All the walls, all the fortifications. They are all stone. Most of their men are in the quarry, and the rest are hauling the stone back and forth."

Trent looked up. His eyes had softened, some of the edge gone out of his shoulders. "I-I didn't think about that."

The air tasted fresh and sweet, the dust knocked down and the tang of it washed away. "There are a lot of things we don't think about." The sheet of rain had turned into a pounding. "It's lightening up. Come on, back to the workshop."

As they left the rain was lessening. It still soaked into his clothes, cold pinpricks that made him walk faster.

"Welcome back," Ned said. Sam shook the water from his back and hands, slicking back his hair.

Trent stamped his feet and scraped the mud off his boots with the side of the porch post.

"Back in for the rest of the day, it looks like." Ned stretched and got up, joining him to look out at the rain. Sam looked down at him. There was an interesting look on his face.

"Yes, I'm afraid. More rain."

"Storm on the horizon. And not just rain." Lightning flashed, lighting up Ned's face. The rumble of thunder came less than a second later.

"Too much. We have too much to do."

"There will always be more to do," Ned said, eyes scanning the horizon. "We must do what we can now, in this time, and let go of the rest."

Sam shook his head. "I wish I had your confidence. I'm not even sure what I'm doing now has any impact on anything other than the few things that are added to the castle."

"We do our part, just as others do theirs."

Sam looked back into the workshop, watching the carpenters at their work. The scrape of a plane, the song of the saw in Kerien's hands. The sound of an offcut falling to the dust. "What am I doing here, in this place?" he wondered aloud.

Ned laughed, making him look in surprise. "That, my boy, is a question we all search for. Even me." He returned to his work with a chuckle, and Sam glanced out into the rain before going to his own workbench.

He had a panel mid carving, a crest of Hornblood with the Tree of Everling embossed on a field of white. He had already carved out the trunk, and most of the branches had come from it, but he had yet to carve the rest.

Taking up his gouge, he sat on the stool, then moved it for better light, and set the tip into the edge of a cut half finished.

The v shaped blade cut into the wood, pulling it away with a light pressure from his hand. He looked back up at his example carving, and traced the branch all the way out to the edge, lessening his pressure and bringing the blade up to a shallower cut.

At the end only a whisper of wood parted from the panel, and he pulled it away to fall to the ground behind him.

He thought as he carved, taking solace in the act as he always did. This was the skill that earned him his master. A steady hand and even pressure with a blade allowed him to work quickly, but precisely.

He had finished most of the tree when the rain slowed to a light patter, then stopped. Drips ran off the roof of the workshop, sloping to the covered porch and falling into puddles below that ran back down the yard and out to the muddy street beyond.

The air was cool now, and fresh. It would have been sweet except for the smell of the mud. Sam kept working, up until the bell of dinner.

"Master Freeman, shall we return to the castle?"

"Not yet," he said, brushing shavings off his work and his pants. "The clouds give me pause. We'll see what tomorrow holds."

Trent turned and walked, joining the others for dinner. Sam let them go ahead, inspecting their work.

Kerien rushed too much, and it showed up in his work. There were plane tracks on the door and saw marks from a careless cut near the tenon. Sam shook his head, another problem he had to deal with. If he would slow down, he would be better than most journeymen, but like this, he could barely be called one.

The paths were muddy as he walked to dinner, his boots squelching with every step. The ground clung to him, refused to let him go.

There was a part of him that was still searching for something, after so many years on this journey. He longed to know what it was, that he could find a way to get there.

Dinner was more of the same, and he kept to himself. He listened to the others talking, then slipped into the shadows to observe.

The talk was muted now, although there was plenty of it. Hushed tones filled the nooks and crannies of the Square as the sun cast its sunset upon the breaking storm clouds.

"More work tomorrow, and what with the winter coming, they'll be pushing us harder than we ever had to work before." The speaker was a mason, one of the older ones on the crew,

Danny. He was just off to one side of the lean to Sam had taken refuge in.

"Do you think they'll do it?" That was Rosco, another mason. Sam frowned to hear his voice. He was one of the ones with Bill today.

"It's only a matter of time. You can believe that we'll be the first targets too."

"Well, at least the walls are up."

"The outer walls. We still have too much work on the keep. If they breach those..."

"We'll be dead no matter, even if the keep is finished."

"Come on, let's go get something to drink." Their conversation faded as they went to the alehouse. Sam guessed they would be refused, unless there was someone on the inside letting them have it.

The memory of the morning came back, burning into his mind. Shame came with it, at not being able to do anything, at not fighting back. He suppressed that.

How had they gotten drunk? Sam thought about following the men, but decided it wasn't worth getting in trouble about. They wouldn't take too kindly to him following them and, after the incident today, it would be best to keep a low profile.

Bill would be in his shack tonight. Sam pondered a visit, wondering if it would do any good. He dismissed it, thinking he might be wise to let him cool off a bit, if the rain and weather hadn't done that for him already.

The weather might put him in a fouler mood, come to think of it. Sam chewed on a piece of grass he plucked from a straggly patch growing beside the Square.

It was trying to survive, just like they were, but there was too much trying to choke it out and kill it. Still, despite all that, it was green and vibrant, a small patch of hope in the dust and mud.

Something came over him seeing it. Sam stood up, brushed off his pants, and walked out of the Square.

He turned right, instead of the left that would bring him back to his shack. In a few more moments he found himself outside Bill's place.

He stopped at the door and waited. Voices drifted out from inside. He wasn't alone.

Sam knocked on the hard door. It gave as he did, then went back to its original position. The voices stopped at once.

"Who is it?" Bill asked.

"Sam."

A pause. Shuffling. The door creaked open half an inch. "What do you want?"

Sam spread out his hands. "To talk. Nothing else."

Bill peered at him with a suspicious eye. The smell of ale drifted from the opening. Sam doubted he would let him in, thought he might slam the door in his face.

Then he swung it open and let him in. "Come in." His face was hard, but Sam went in anyway. Another mason, Barry he thought, stood in the corner. Sam entered, then Bill shut the door behind him.

Bill went back to his stool and sat. "I'm listening."

"I've done something to offend you, haven't I?" Sam stopped in front of Bill. He glanced at the table, a few mugs on the corner. Empty, but enough foam in two to be recently full.

A smile blossomed on Bill's face, then he laughed. "Done something? Yes, you've done something. Done nothing but hinder our work is what you've done."

"When have I done that?"

"You drag your feet, take forever with the beam-work, then dare to come in and deny it?" Bill leaned back, but Sam wasn't convinced it was from ease. "Impolite, I'd say."

"I'd agree. Quite disagreeable," Barry said, walking around.

"We've set the beams when you've asked." Sam crossed his arms, trying to suppress his anger.

"So now it's our fault?"

"That's not what I said," Sam said. He was beginning to regret coming. A hint of frustration crept into his voice, no matter how much he tried to hide it. He took a deep breath. "Perhaps we could work together more closely so that I'd know where you need us the most. We don't have enough men right now."

Bill sat up straight, eyes flashing. "You don't have enough men? What do you think we have, men aplenty?"

"I know you don't have enough either — "

"Don't you come in here telling us what we have or have not," Bill cut him off. He was straight on the stool now, practically on the edge.

Barry had edged behind him, and Sam took a look at him from the side of his vision. "I came for peace, not for anger." Although anger is what he was feeling.

"Peace? You came for peace?" Bill let out a snort of laughter.

Rough hands seized Sam from behind. Bill thrust his face into Sam's, his hot, alcohol soaked breath oozing over him. "You came to a fortress of the war for peace?"

Torches fluttered in the night, and horses stamped. The Bear stepped up into the saddle, then hauled his hulking frame on. The straps creaked ominously, but held. He swung the black horse around and faced the group of onlookers.

"Tonight we ride for glory and the blood that will flow like rain." Smiles appeared, then a round of cheers went up from the rough-looking group of fighting men. He wished he had more, but a few dozen men would be more than enough. There were enough the torchlight didn't touch the far edge of their numbers. "We will catch them by surprise and make them fear the men of Belmarch once again."

"Like sheep, they would be led to the slaughter and we will leave their bones for the vultures to pick over. You will have your fill of their women and drink the tears of their sorrow." Another round of cheers, and he turned and galloped off into the night. The men followed.

The sound of thunderous horseflesh rose into the night sky, devoid of a moon and black as night. The Bear smiled as he thought of the castle they were to crush, and how easy it would be.

5

UNWELCOME NEWS

The first hit landed above his ribcage, the second in his stomach. His air left, and Sam doubled over.

Barry held him up. Gasping, Sam struggled for breath. When he caught it he stood back up.

"Not so proud now, are you?" Bill snarled. Barry laughed at him.

"Don't hit me."

Bill's eyes widened. "What was that?"

"I said don't hit me." Sam kept his voice quiet, but let the edge of danger into it. It gave Bill some pause, even in his inebriated state.

Barry pulled at his arms, tightening them and hurting his shoulders. His chest hurt, and his stomach throbbed. Bill had strength, he had to give him that.

Their eyes locked. Sam held his gaze and his head upright. There was a desperation in Bill's eyes, and it surprised him.

At last, Bill looked away. "Let him go."

"Boss — "

"I said let him go. He isn't worth it. Just a nobody trying to make a name for himself."

Barry let go after a vicious tweak. Sam rotated his arms. "We're done here."

"It would be easier if we worked together," Sam said, holding hope of one last thing that would let them work together.

Bill thought for a moment, then there was a knock at the door. "Get out," Bill said.

Sam left, knowing it was no use. Men with more mugs brimming with ale stepped aside as he walked out the door.

He brushed between them, ignoring the ugly looks they gave him.

Night was full now, and dark. The lessening light of the Square guided him home, although he walked past his own bed and down the road to the woods.

The sounds of laughter and conversation died down as he walked, replaced with the crickets music. His arms still hurt from being held.

He went to sleep, troubled and wishing he were somewhere else. Had he made the wrong decision? Was he supposed to be somewhere else?

The last thought he had was that he could leave it all behind, go somewhere else, and learn something new.

The next morning brought strange news. Crowds gathered in the Square as he got ready, the murmuring from their conversation seemed unusual for this early.

Sam walked outside, only to be sucked into the crowd. "What's happening?"

"The Overseer's coming down. Something big is happening," said Luke, a farmer.

Sam looked over to the other carpenters, gathered up beside the cooking fire that smoldered in the morning light. Someone should have been tending it, but it had died down.

Cold food lay forgotten on the tables, and Sam pushed his way through the crowd to take a cake and munch on it while he listened.

"This is too early to let us go. Why are they bringing us together?" Sally said. She was rocking her baby and clutching him to her chest. Her husband tried to calm her.

"We'll find out shortly. Here they come now."

He was right, the Overseer entered the Square, flanked by guards and with the young man Sam had seen in his room. The crowd shouted questions at him, and the Overseer raised his hands.

"Quiet, quiet now. Everybody calm down." The Overseer mopped his head with a handkerchief. His forehead shone. "Now, I've called you all here to introduce his highness Duke Evan Hornblood, the third of his name." He stepped aside and let the young man enter the circle. A hushed crowd watched him.

The Overseer bowed, and the group followed. Appeased, the young man gave a half smile and cleared his throat. "Thank you all for being here and the work that you do. It is so very important that this fortress be completed. Our very way of life is at stake and depends on it. The Belmarch are on the move, no longer content to fight amongst themselves." A murmur rushed through the crowd, and the Overseer gave them a nasty look. It died back down.

"I'm sure you all have worked hard up until now, but I'm afraid I'm going to ask you to work a little harder. This is Captain Yand." He motioned to his companion, a tall, muscular man with a short haircut and a peppering of salt at his temples. "He will be training you all in rudimentary combat."

The Overseer broke in as the crowd started to raise questions. "You will not be expected to fight. This is just a basic precaution. The world is dangerous and we all know what the Belmarch raiders can do, eh?"

The question stuck, and the Overseer again yielded to Earl Hornblood, who nodded in a dismissive way. "No, you won't be fighting," he said, irritated. "But you will be ready to defend her. The garrison takes up residence in the next two months, and will be sent upriver soon. In the meantime, we'll secure the castle and move everything we can inside the walls."

"It sounds like you expect an attack," someone yelled out. The Earl's head swung to the sound, examining the crowd, but the voice was lost.

"We expect nothing. We plan for the worst. The Hornbloods wouldn't have held the northern province this long if we hadn't. Captain."

"At the third bell, you'll be expected to meet me in the castle courtyard. Men, that is," the captain said, gazing over the assembled ragtag group of workers and their families. "We'll work on basic fighting first, then long arms next. Any man caught shirking his duty will be set to the pole and lashed."

His steely eyes looked them over. Not a peep was heard. "Does anyone have a problem with that?" He dropped the volume of his voice to a low whisper. Sam thought he could hear everyone swallowing, but inside, he smiled. This man was hard.

But he also expected him to fight. Sam roiled inside. How was he going to get out of this? Would they take more work as an excuse?

Or maybe that he had to oversee others, that he didn't have time to train.

While he was thinking about this, he had missed more of the conversation, and the Hornblood was talking again.

"There will be rewards for every man, woman, and child for the successful completion of Hornblood Castle. We will be the fortress on the hill, the defender of Chathem, the savior of our people." His eyes flashed as he said it. Sam didn't buy it. "So go forth and do your duty." With that, he swung around, trailing his cloak in a flourish, and left. The captain was at his side, but the Overseer scrambled with his guards.

"Back to work, like he said," the Overseer said as he tripped up the path behind the others.

"Trained to fight, are they mad?" Trent said, rushing up to him. "Why are they doing that?"

"You heard the man, just a precaution," Sam said, taking another bite of his cake. It was cold, but still good. Made with caring hands.

His lack of family was pronounced then, as the men who had them rushed off to talk with them. Husbands led their wives by the elbows, or were led just as much, and they spoke in hushed tones.

Martha practically dragged her husband by the ear, giving him a mouthful. Suddenly, that family situation didn't seem as bad.

Still, the pain in his heart continued, even as Trent followed him to the others. None of the carpenters that remained had families except Archie. "Take some time to talk it over," Sam said, seeing the look in his eyes.

Gratefulness replaced the anxiety, and he left to find his wife Beth and their young girl Nancy. "The rest of us are going back to work. We'll pick up the slack in the line until he gets back."

"I don't want to fight," Trent said, sitting down and crossing his arms.

What was he supposed to say? Sam looked at him, feeling exactly what he was feeling, only without the memories to accompany them.

"Ned, you'll finish the door?"

"Quicker'n two shakes." Ned winked at him and sauntered off with Kerien, whistling a tune to mock him as he went.

"I thought you wanted to fight," Sam said, rounding on Trent. "Or do you just want others to fight for you?"

"That's not fair."

"Neither will the enemy, whoever they are, when they show up here with axe and sword. They'll take your life faster than you can give it up." He softened his tone and dropped to one knee. "I don't like it either. Give it some time, it sounds like it will only be for a month or two and then the fighters will get here. I don't think they'll waste time drilling fighting stances into carpenter's apprentices when that happens."

Trent turned red. "I don't know how to fight."

"You do, in a way. We all do, when we need to." He got back up. "Come on, to work. The first bell's already rung."

They walked side by side through the hardening mud, and Sam watched the sky. The storm had passed and left sunny skies. It would dry everything out and keep it ready to work.

But now he found himself dragged back to fighting. He had come here to escape it, not to get a bigger dose and with less protection.

The others were working, and Sam put on his apron and took up his plane. He stared down at it, a tool of iron and wood.

How was cutting through wood any different than cutting through a man? It bled sap, it was a living creature.

He set it to the plank and pushed. A thin, clean shaving curled up into a circle until his plane went off the end.

Sam's fingers wrapped around it. It was thin, delicate, and smooth. One quick crush and it crackled beneath his grip, then fell as he let it loose.

"Kerien, please come over here." Kerien stopped his work, halfway through a saw cut, and set down his tools. His brows were knit together in a question.

"Yes?"

Sam offered him the plane. "Take a cut for me."

Kerien took it and set it on the board. He pushed, keeping his hand steady under Sam's watchful eye. When he was done Sam rubbed his hand along the cut and sighted down the edge with a square.

There was no gap. "Good." Kerien smiled as Sam straightened. "Now why can't you do that on your own?" Sam kept his voice down, a low whisper meant for Kerien's ears only.

His smile vanished into a frown. The others kept working, seemingly oblivious of the interaction.

"What do you mean?"

"Shall we examine your current work?"

He dropped his gaze, his frown deepening. "No."

"You're a good journeyman when watched. Am I to be here every second of the day to do it?" Sam looked at him. "How many do we have that can?"

"No, you don't need to," Kerien mumbled.

"I didn't think I did. You're on your way to the master's trail, but I'm afraid you'll never make it with the quality of work you have now."

"You want me to work fast."

"I want you to work well."

"But there's too few of us and too much to do."

Sam held up a hand. "Let me worry about who does what and how many we have to work. How many hours of the day do you have to worry about it?"

Kerien shrugged.

"None." Sam ran a hand through his hair, greasy and unwashed. He would need to visit the river soon, if he could ever find time. "I need you to focus on the work you have now, and let me worry about the rest. Deal?"

"I guess."

"It that doesn't work for you we can change places." Sam let a hint of a smile play across his face.

"No," Kerien said with a grimace, "you can keep it."

"Good man." Sam squeezed his arm. "You're getting stronger than anyone in here. I'll have you putting up the beams soon. Go on now, back to work."

Kerien, properly chastened, went back to his bench. He kept his saw straight, paying attention to his line.

Sam hoped it would hold. He wondered if he had done the right thing, but then quickly dismissed the thought.

He would protect all of them, as much as he was able. Sam picked up the plane again and stared down at it. They were his family.

6

MISTAKES

The afternoon sun beat down on them, pulling out the sweat from his body and burning his skin. Sam struggled with one end, the rope creaking dangerously.

"Down now." He tried to guide the end in as Trent unwound the crane. The beam came down, swung wide, then corrected with Sam's guidance.

It set down into the rock, falling within the hole the masons had made for them, and he sighed. "Keep going."

The crane sang, then the beam stopped. The rope went slack. Sam stared down the edge.

One side had gone in well, all the way into the rock and seated exactly where he planned.

This end, as he expected, was stuck halfway in. Over an inch of wood stuck up over the rock, where it should have been under the edge.

"Back up." Trent gave an exasperated look to him, but worked the wheel of the crane in the other direction. The rope pulled taut, then strained and broke the beam free. "Stop."

He looked on both sides, feeling along the edge. There it was, a shiny side and smoother than the rest. A few swipes of his chisel took off the offending wood, and a few steps above for good measure.

When he finished, he looked out over the edge of the castle wall. The green trees covered the edge of the river, but it wouldn't be long until they would be able to see it properly.

From up here you could hear it, a rushing, bubbling noise that was lost unless you really thought about it.

It was the shallowest spot in the Venti for miles, and the best place to cross it. As soon as they were done with the castle the trees would come down on that side, leaving the defenders an easy arrow shot for anyone trying to ford.

The King's men had done well in their selection, although they had torn down an old wooden tower that functioned as the warning for the Chathem defenders in the past.

Masons crawled over the walls of the keep, cutting stone, setting stone, mixing mortar. He couldn't escape the sound of them anywhere, no matter how hard he tried.

Trent lowered the crane again, and this time the beam set in perfectly. Sam ran his hands along the edge, feeling the rise of the stone and the lip that would allow the masons to encase the end in mortar and continue up the next course.

"Now, for the cross members." They were cut and at the bottom, and it meant a long walk down the stairs and through the keep to get there. Trent started lowering the rope of the crane while Sam started down.

The sunlight diminished as he walked down, covered up by the construction above. He paused for a moment in the cool of the corridor below to rest.

Voices drifted from somewhere down the hall. He couldn't help but catch what they were saying.

"We won't get them now. The raiders in the west threaten us more every day. They kill villagers, disrupt trade, and seize as much as they want."

"But even with the Belmarch on the move?"

"The spies tell us they march to fight each other, not us. We'll be safe enough with the walls finished."

"I don't like it." Sam caught himself listening, then moved away, back the other direction, toward the door. The Overseer continued to talk. "You saw them. They aren't fighters, they'll cave the instant someone threatens them."

"Leave that to Captain — " The words drifted away, cut short as he closed the door behind him. That had been the young Hornblood.

Something wasn't right. These men were untested, untried, except for the man they brought with them. Why would they even think about training us?

He didn't have time to think about it though, Trent was waiting. Heat hit him as he left the keep, and the rope was down on the ground and ready.

Sam tied them up, then guided the beam as much as he could until it was too high to reach. He watched it swing for a moment, then went back up the same way he had come down.

The conversation was quieter, too quiet for him to hear now. He felt ashamed that he hadn't left earlier, but even more unsettled by what he had heard.

Trent was swinging the crane into position when he came up, and Sam joined him to push it. It squealed, but gave with enough force, and the beam was soon dangling.

"Line it up first. We've got to get that tenon in the mortise, then set the beam in the wall." Sam picked his way over the unfinished masonry, walking along the thick two-foot wall. Two courses of stone were held together with mortar and connecting spans, which made for tricky movement but thick fortifications.

"Ready?" Trent asked. Sam braced his legs and took hold of the leader rope, pulling gently to swing the wall end toward him.

"Lower it down." The beam dropped until it was about six inches above the wall. "Hold it there."

Sam tipped it up and fought with the end to sight the tenon. It took more effort than he expected, but eventually he hooked it into the mortised hole in the main beam. "Lower it."

Trent let it down slowly, and Sam guided it into the waiting slot in the stone. This time, it slipped in perfectly.

Another test of the fingers, and it was just under the edge. "Good, we'll get the other."

The first had gone well, and he hoped the other would, too. Then he could give the tower back to Bill and the masons to finish, if they would take it.

The next one went up faster, and they were just getting into place when a familiar face showed up.

Trent looked worried. That was his first indication. Sam glanced behind him, checking the last connection to see Bill.

He was alone. That was a good sign. The air hung damp and swollen, not a hint of wind in sight, even up as high as they were.

It was an oppressive heat, and one he was going to be glad to escape. "Afternoon, Bill."

"You finally finished?" Bill walked over to examine their handiwork. "I thought you wouldn't be able to use this after the...fall it had taken."

"Oh, she isn't so fragile as that to be bloodied by a token beating." Sam patted the thick oak. "She's made of sterner stuff. You'll see." A hint of his anger leaked through, and Sam winced.

He had to control himself, if no one else would.

Bill sniffed, then dragged his dirty shoe along its surface. "Too high. You'll have to carve out more for us to work around. Take it out and do it again."

Sam's smile froze on his face. "There's plenty of room for you to work."

"Need an inch or more. You know that."

"That's not-" Trent began, but Sam cut him off with a quick motion of his hand.

"Need an excuse to catch up on some work, then?" He thought about poking him, mentioning something about his haggard look or his unkempt hair. The bags under his eyes might have done it. "Fine. Feel free to blame me."

"The Overseer's patience is wearing thin with you," Bill said, kicking the side of the beam. It didn't move. Sam was hoping his toe broke, but he seemed fine. "One of these day's you'll answer for your shoddy work."

That poked him, and it cut deep. Sam clamped his mouth shut, teeth grinding against one another. He stood and carefully picked his way to the stairs. After a few deep breaths he regained control. "Come Trent. WE have work to do."

"Just going to run away?" Bill stood at the top of the stairs, barring the way. He had gotten there fast, but he knew his way around the stone like the back of his hand. He wasn't the Master Mason for nothing.

"Going to do my job, just like you suggested." Sam tried to step around, but Bill stayed in his way. Sweat trickled down the back of his neck, tickling him. "I can't do it while I'm up here."

"Go ahead, go down. Abandon the work you have to do here. Word will get around." Bill moved in close, mere inches from their noses touching. "I know what kind of man you are. A coward," he whispered.

"Think whatever you like." Sam was cloaking himself now in the old techniques he had learned as a young child. His body was covered in mail, just like he imagined it. Each word was an arrow that bounced off. Sam nodded.

Trent walked past them. Sam stood his ground, matching Bill eye to eye. There was that same look, deep down one of desperation.

Finally, Bill relented. He stepped back, easing the menacing closeness, and waved a hand in front of him. "An early dinner is best for the cowards."

"One day I hope you can learn to trust me." Sam started down the stairs, then stopped and looked back. "First, you'll have to trust yourself."

Without another word, he turned and followed Trent, leaving Bill shocked at the top of the stairs.

Sam had no doubt Bill would tell the Overseer that he had shirked his duty, made a fool of the masons, and failed to give them enough room to work. The Overseer would listen and believe it. What did he know about masonry or woodwork?

He was an aristocrat, fallen out of favor low enough to be sent here but high enough to be treated as a serious man. Whatever he had done in his past life did not lend well to him building a castle, but he was the only one they had.

Sam considered his options as they were swallowed up into the merely warm innards of the keep. He didn't know of anything other than to go about his business as usual.

Going to the Overseer first would seem petty, like he was trying to shift blame from his own actions to someone else. Exactly what Bill wanted.

But on the other hand, waiting for Bill to tell his tale the way he wanted was also a losing proposition.

He was stuck in between a rock and the wall.

"Master, why don't you go to the Overseer and tell him what's happening?" Trent asked.

The boy had picked up on it. Sam wasn't surprised, but he did wish it wasn't as obvious as it was.

"Sometimes you need to pick your battles. Right now I don't curry much favor with the Overseer. Anything would be unwelcome coming from me."

"So why don't you have it come from someone else?"

Sam shook his head. "I'm afraid that's what will happen. Don't worry about this, it shouldn't concern you." But it did, and Sam knew he couldn't keep it from him, nor the others.

He trailed his hands along the stone, bumping over the rough edges and projections of the inner wall. How would he have handled this in the past?

With his fists, probably. But that was a long time ago, and this was a different life. Even now he felt the creature within him stirring, the one that craved blood. Loved it, desired it.

Wanted it more than anything else in the world.

Unleashing that creature would mean going back to a dark place that he had sworn off long ago.

A thought struck him. Trent had mentioned having it come from someone else, but not him.

Was it possible that was the right answer after all?

They reached the bottom landing and entered the hallway. The workshop was to the right.

"Take the tools back to the workshop. I have something I need to do." Sam handed him his tools, turning deeper into the keep.

"Master?"

"Go, do as you're told. And tell the others they need to hurry up with their work, too."

Sam went left down the hall, turned right, then passed the Overseer's room. He kept going until he was at the one room that had been completed.

Sam raised his fist and knocked.

Despite his large frame, the Bear was quiet as he crept on all fours up to the edge of the small rise to the thin man that laid there.

"Over to the right," he said with a rasp, his vocal cords damaged in battle long ago. The Bear followed his outstretched hand, shifting slightly and rustling the leaves. The forest floor smelled of damp and growing mushrooms.

There it was, a slight dark gray protruding from the treetops on the other side. As he watched a man appeared at the top and moved around.

"What are they doing?"

"Building. They've been adding stone all morning."

The Bear grunted. The river was swollen with the rain, bits of trees and other debris floating by. Too high to ford, for now.

"Keep watch," the Bear said, then turned and crept down the hill to the waiting band of his lieutenants. "We're early enough to catch them unaware. As soon as the river lets up, we'll cross and attack."

7

HUNG JOURNEY

At first Sam thought no one was in, but a sound of movement inside made his heart beat. Footsteps crossed the room, then the door opened.

"What is it?" The young Hornblood peered out from a crack. "What do you want?"

"I'm here to measure for your room, Sire." Sam gave a customary bow.

"Very well then." He opened the door up. "Come in."

"Thank you." Sam entered. It was the brightest room in the keep, and the best furnished. Most of the furniture had been carted in, but some of it he recognized from the workshop.

Now that he was inside, he wasn't exactly sure what to do. he had to plant some measure of respect for himself if he was going to have any chance of surviving the next few months.

His eyes wandered around the room as he pulled out the measuring stick he kept in his pocket.

The young Hornblood was returning to his desk, and when he got there, he picked up the papers that were on it and slipped into the chair with a heavy sigh.

He put one elbow on the table and held up the papers to the light of the windows, reading.

A few chairs, a table filled with wine and a plate of leftover food, with flies buzzing around it, and a nice carpet made up the rest of the room.

Sam walked over to the window, measuring along its surface. He tried to be quiet and not disturb the Duke, but he would have to talk to him if this was going to work.

But what about?

Two spans on the bottom. Sam checked the thickness of the sill.

It wasn't going to work if he kept this up, not like this. *What was I thinking, coming in here like this?*

He turned back to the door. Why he thought this would work, he didn't know.

Then he saw something that might work.

Sam walked over to the desk and stood in front of it. He waited a few respectfully moments, but when he was ignored, he cleared his throat.

The Duke looked up, a hint of irritation flashing in his brown eyes. "What is it?"

"Where would you like the crest, Sire?"

"What?"

"Your family crest. Would you like it here," Sam pointed to the front of the desk, "or there?" He pointed to the wall above the duke.

The Duke looked, then paused. "Which one would be better?"

"If I may?" Sam waited until he nodded. "The desk would give your visitors something to look at below, but above you, we can carve it much larger and make it more...imposing, if you will. They would be reminded of the strength of the house of Hornblood and the representative that has come here."

The Duke's mouth curled up at the corner, and his eyes lit up. "On the wall then."

"Very good, Sire. Please excuse me." Sam was relieved he never asked why he had to take these measurements now, but he took three spans for the opening, and guessed another three up would do.

A crest that would certainly be imposing. Now, he just had to figure out how to make it.

"By your leave." Sam returned to the door.

Duke Hornblood waved a hand. "Dismissed."

"Good evening, Sire."

He shut the door behind him with a click. A list was running through his mind, and he couldn't produce everything on it.

That meant one person had to be visited.

He set off at a brisk walk, checking the sun as he left the keep. The heat blasted him as he did, pushing away the stuffiness of inside and making him suck in a deep breath of the wet air.

The taste of stone dust came with it. The masons were still at work on the keep, raising the top before they would move on to continue the towers.

But Sam turned right, ignoring the path back to the workshop, and headed for the constant sound of ringing and the smoke rising above a stone structure in the shade of the wall.

Two ends were open, the others made of stone on one side and the wall on the other.

He thought the heat outside was uncomfortable, but as he stepped into the shade of the blacksmith, he was glad he didn't work in there.

It smelled like coal, metal, and oil. The smiths were working, one hammering at a hunk of iron.

"Dale, good afternoon." Sam raised a hand to him.

"What brings you in here?" Dale's muscles rippled as he continued to hammer, turning the chisel over each time. He barely gave him a glance.

"Special order."

"Oh?"

"Call it a favor." Sam leaned against a post and waited for him to finish. When Dale did, he raised an eyebrow and dumped the chisel in the quenching bucket beside him.

It sizzled and raised a puff of steam. That chisel was destined for the masons, to be worn down against rock until it needed to be sharpened once again.

Dale wiped off his hands on his apron, then went over to a bucket of water. He splashed some on his face. "Special how?"

"I need some nails to hang a crest."

"I'll have Brent make you some."

"These aren't normal nails. I'll need them to be three inches long." Sam thought for a moment. "Make that four inches."

"What are you trying to hang, a horse?" Sam didn't realize Dale's eyebrows could go that high.

"Something like that. A whole tree." He would have to find the right wood. Something that matched, didn't overpower the crest, and was strong enough to last. And large enough. "And I need it by tomorrow."

"Now Sam, you know I have too much to do."

"We all do." Sam knew that Dale needed at least three apprentices to keep up with the work. He had two. Another smith would be better. "I think Bill and the masons feel it, too."

"Don't get me started on Bill." The big man's eyebrows dug into his brow now, and his voice took an already deep voice two shades deeper.

Something to think about. Another ally.

"You're having issues with him, too?"

"Only every other day. Bringing me broken tools, chisels so blunted it takes twice as long to sharpen them. Bah." He spit out on the dirt, then wiped his mouth and beard. "I think they break them on purpose, at how bad they look."

"Come to think of it, we've seen an increase in handles lately." Sam shook his head. Another stalling tactic? "Regardless, this would help me out. I'd owe you a favor."

"And that would make how many?"

"Too many?" Sam couldn't help but smile, and the big man laughed a deep belly laugh.

"I'll be calling on you soon, someday. If I can ever get away from this work."

"I hear you. Mayhaps with the Duke in the castle, things might turn around."

"Or maybe I'd mount a hog and ride it into the sunset. You didn't hear that, boys. And get back to work." His apprentices had taken a keen ear and somehow their work had slowed down.

"Let me refit your hammer for you."

"Not a chance. I'll use that until it breaks into driftwood into my hands." Dale gave him a look that made Sam think he was considering breaking him.

"If you reconsider..."

"You're the first one I'll come to."

Dale mopped the sweat from his face. "Go on, leave me to my work."

"I will. Let me know when you need that favor." Sam turned and walked back to the workshop, letting his feet take him as he thought.

He wasn't the only one. Somehow, this was reassuring and aggravating all at once. What was driving Bill to this? And why did it have to be now, when so much was left to do?

The smoke of dinner wafted up over the village and the workshop, meeting him along the way. Baking bread and beans.

Sam was looking forward to one, and not so much to the other. They'd had so much of it before the families had come.

It was easy, and fed them well, but day after day they had grown tiresome.

Trent was back, and already hard at work, when he entered the yard. Sam walked among the stacks of lumber, separated to dry out, and tried to find something that would do.

It was difficult to find something so large in span. There were a few that came close, but nothing to what he wanted.

While he thought about it, an eagle circled overhead, screaming as it scanned the farms and fields below. Red as clay, a Firetail Eagle.

A few lazy flaps of its wings took it higher, in a great circle. The tail feathers twisted and fluttered as the great wings held steady, his shadow running along the ground.

Likely scaring away all the other things it was looking for.

Sam let it fly, taking the largest and driest of the sawn planks. It took him a while to dig it out from the bottom of a stack, but soon enough, he had it free.

It had cupped a little, but not much. The heartwood ran down the center, quartersawn.

A few scrapes of a plane revealed the grain. Straight and unobtrusive oak. Just what he needed.

But, it was too small, by just a hair. The dinner bell rang.

"Looking for something specific?" Ned asked as they filed out.

"Yes, a special project."

"How special?" Sam looked to the others.

"Go on, get your food." When they had gone, trudging down the path to the Square, Sam relayed his plan.

"Do you think it will work?"

"It's a gamble," Ned said, rubbing his chin. "But if you think it's worth the time, then I'll support you on it."

"Thanks. Now, if this was a few inches longer, it might do."

"Frame it up." The thought struck him like a thunderbolt. Why hadn't he thought of that? Sam grabbed Ned in a hug.

"You've saved me a great deal of trouble. Here I was, thinking we had to bring down the biggest tree in the forest when it was right in front of me the whole time. That's perfect."

"If you're going for imposing, it won't hurt."

"I'll take this in, go ahead. I'll catch up." Sam dragged the wood into the workshop and muscled it onto his bench. A few hours dressing, another couple of carving, and then some joinery.

He could do it all in a day or two, on top of his other work. It might not be soon enough, though.

Dinner was as he expected, and he chewed the beans without tasting them, planning everything out in his head. Some smaller carvings would work well on the frame, something to stroke the ego, perhaps?

The time went quicker than he expected, and the third bell was ringing. Workers dropped off their plates, but instead of going to their houses, they turned up to the castle.

At first, Sam was puzzled, then he remembered.

The fighting.

They were going up to the castle, to the large training ground that was currently being used to stage materials.

And there they would be forced to learn to fight.

His stomach churned at the thought. He couldn't do it, no matter the consequence.

But everyone else was going, and the other carpenters were looking back at him.

He had an example to set.

Ned raised an eyebrow at him.

"Well, off we go." This would eat into his working time, too. He dropped his empty bowl and spoon off with the washer-women and followed the others in the fading light.

Each step was heavy, each footfall bringing him closer to a decision he didn't want to make.

But behind him, the carpenters followed. He had to set an example.

The question was, what example was he going to set?

8

TRAINING

They trickled into the dusty yard. Captain Yand stood at the top, watching them. His gaze was steely and his posture was even harder.

Sam slipped to the back once they were there. Bill, he noticed, was leading the group of masons at the front of the pack.

Sam rubbed his belly. The pain had gone away, for the most part, but the bruises remained. Dark, purple welts of a reminder of who Bill really was.

He seemed attentive and watchful. Sam wondered if it was all a ploy to get the attention of the fighter, to use it to his advantage like everything else these days.

"Listen up, boys," Yand's voice boomed, echoing against the castle walls and reverberating. "This is no time for fooling around. I've been given a task to make men out of you maggots." At this, he clasped his hands behind his back and started to stride in front of them in a big loop. "I'm afraid I don't have much time of it either. So you'll have to listen closely. Those who don't will be punished."

At this, he turned. The group, so animated and conversational walking in, was now quiet. Sam thought he could have heard a blade of grass drop.

It emphasized the quiet of twilight that had drawn over them like a blanket. Torches burned around them, spitting and flickering. It cast strange shadows, and the fire mesmerized Sam, bringing him back to the past.

"We will go through the basics first. Now, each man pick a partner and face each other." They paired up, and Yand chastened them to move faster.

Sam took Ned. What was he going to do?

"We will learn to punch, then kick, then throw. First up, the punch." Yand squared up to them, brought his fists up, and demonstrated a punch in the air. "Put force behind it with your hips. Now, you all try."

Sam stood and watched as they punched the air around him. He looked down at his hand, tightening it in a fist.

The world seemed to shrink and lessen. His hand shook. His blood pounded. Breath came in short, quick gasps.

I can't do it. I won't do it.

"You there." The crowd turned to him. The world rushed back to Sam, and he looked up.

Right into the cold eyes of Captain Yand.

"What are you doing?"

Sam's mouth went dry.

"Answer me. Why don't you do what I tell you?"

"I can't." It came out in a whisper. Men around him whispered.

"Did I hear you right? You refuse to do what I said?" Captain Yand stalked up to him, parting the crowd like a blade cutting through flesh. In two more steps, he stood, looming up over Sam.

"I've done what was asked. I've come here by your order." Sam knew he was treading on ice. "I can't fight."

Yand's eyes narrowed. "You'll fight, and you'll do as you're told."

"I will build, I will labor, but I will not fight." Sam dropped his gaze, steeling himself for whatever was to come. "Please."

Snickers ran through the masons. He thought he heard whispers of "coward" in them.

"Keep quiet." Yand turned back to Sam. "Look me in the eye."

Sam raised his gaze and did as he was told. For a moment Yand only looked, examining him, tearing him apart, flaying his mind. He reached into his head and seized his soul.

"Very well then. You all heard this man, he refuses to fight. Well, then, you all bear witness to those who refuse to do as they are instructed." He waved a hand. A man came forward, carrying two pails of on a beam.

Yand snapped, and he put the beam on Sam's back. Sam accepted his fate, took it willingly.

"He'll stand here and bear the weight of his decision." Yand nodded to another. Two men came out, pails full of water. "Not a single drop spilled while we train. To remind you of the weight you bear. The weight of the Kingdom, the protection of it. Not just in how you fight, but in how you build."

One by one, the men added the buckets to the beam. They were heavy, filled to the top. Sam bore the load, glad that this was it.

So far.

"Now, all of you — back to work. Show me your punches, and practice on each other." The men did as they were told, leaving Sam to stand bearing the weight of the water.

Although the water wasn't heavy, it did eat into his shoulders. Sam stood and watched the others as they learned the bare, rudimentary fighting techniques that wouldn't save them in a fight.

If he was going to be serious about this, they should have been learning to use knives and bows. They couldn't stand up to seasoned fighters that would be in a raiding party.

The heat of the day had lessened, but it wasn't gone. Sweat ran down his head, and Sam started to feel the ache of the beam across his shoulders. It bit into him, pressed into him.

It had been a long day already, with hard work. Sam was used to it, though, and he took it in stride.

He breathed and closed his eyes. They kept training, they kept learning. Yand moved on to kicking, then a combination of the two.

"You all need to think about these moves, what you would do in the heat of battle." Yand walked around the heavy breathing men. "When you are fighting for your life you have no time to think, only react. Now, we move on to sparring."

The pairs were faced off, and a few guards that were part of the Overseer's muscle were scattered through the crowd. Sam was feeling the burning in his legs now, but it looked like they had a long time to go.

"First man to get the other to the ground wins. The loser will deal with something unpleasant."

They fought. Grunts, cries, and the sound of men striking other men drifted into the darkening night.

Ned was thrown to the ground by Archie. Kerien tossed a mason about his size. Trent lost badly.

Bill seemed to be doing well, fighting one of his own men. Or, at least, it looked that way.

When the last contestants had finished, Yand brought up the losers in a line. "For failing, you will each receive one strike. Remember this."

Sam looked away as he brought out a club. One by one, he went down the line. Why was he doing this? What good was it to train the men this way?

They sparred again. This time, most of the losers won. The punishment was repeated. Sam's legs were starting to burn. He shifted his stance.

His back would feel it in the morning, and his neck. There would be a bruise there.

He tried to ignore what was going on in front of him, to think of something else. The first thing that came to mind was home and the river.

The coolness against his skin on a hot day, the way it tasted. Fresh, clear. Infusing him with energy after a swim. The fish that swam along its path.

Sam licked his lips, dry. The heat of the sun had drained him, and now he finally felt its effects.

They wouldn't be as productive tomorrow. Could the Overseer see that?

Probably not.

Sam wondered what he would do when he found out they had fallen behind, because they would fall behind. All of them.

Anger, rage. He expected loud outbursts and following chastisements. But there would be no use trying to tell him what had happened.

The training dragged on well into the night. Men were bruised and battered. Not one had managed to win all their fights, even Bill.

Yand had seen to that.

He shifted the pairs, making sure they were matched up in height and weight as much as possible, and if need be, putting one at a disadvantage.

Finally, he called an end to the training. Sam could almost hear the collective sigh that went through their minds.

"Tomorrow I expect you to do better. Some of you may think that my tactics are harsh. Barbaric." Yand loomed over them, looking each in the eye. "I'll tell you this."

He pointed to the north. "Those men won't treat you with respect. Those men won't pick you up from the ground and pat you on the back. Those men are hardened fighters. They will rip out your throat and leave you bleeding on the ground to get to the next one."

Silence. Somewhere an owl hooted. "I'm preparing you for them. For war. No matter how hard I push you, remember that it is for your life. So that you will survive."

Yand waited. No one said anything. "Dismissed. Get some sleep."

They filed out, bent and wounded. Yand came over to Sam, who had been left off to the side. He let the other men go before he said anything.

"You'll need to fight. Those are the orders."

"I've made my choice," Sam said. His lips cracked.

"Shame. Could have been a good fighter. I would have made something out of you."

Sam smiled ruefully. "I don't think so."

"Drop them."

He shrugged, and the weight came off his shoulders in an instant. Sweet relief, as it splashed on the ground. Sam rubbed his shoulders, trying to get some feeling back into them.

"Most men would have dropped those. At least, most not used to carrying them." Yand was giving him a strange look. "You'll fight tomorrow, or we add more weight. You have tonight to think on it."

"You have my answer." Yand froze mid-step. He had turned away to walk back to the keep. "I won't fight. No matter what you do to me."

"Sam, was it?"

"Yes."

"Good night Sam." Yand turned back and walked off into the night. Sam turned and walked back to his own hut.

The night had cooled now, and his hut was the same temperature.

He could leave. Go somewhere else. But then he would be running again. Always changing, always going somewhere else.

He needed to stay, to finish this. There was a promise he had to keep, both to himself and to others.

Sam sat on the edge of his bed, about to get under the blanket, but he stared out the window to the night and stars beyond.

"Remember, move like lightning, strike like a hammer." Bear stood above the group of fighters arranged before him. The moon shone in the night sky, a half sphere of white. The forest was quiet.

Only the creatures of the night stirred.

And the warriors.

"Our swords are strong," one man said.

"For blood and honor," the others joined him. Every man made his last adjustments, checked his equipment one last time.

Made fast his sword and his knife. Axe and bow.

Bear nodded and turned. He took the first step, crunching through the dead leaves and undergrowth of the forest.

The others followed, just as quiet. The smell of pine and oak was strong here, mixed with the undergrowth they kicked up that was earthy and green.

He walked with anticipation and held one hand to the sword on his hip. Bear's eyes shone in the darkness, not a single torch in sight.

They reached the shore of the river within a few minutes. It trickled and murmured, no longer swollen with the rain.

The mud sucked at his boots, but Bear pushed on. A quick splash and he was in. The others followed into the cold, crippling water.

At the deepest point, it went up to their chests. This was the time of most danger. The tower was higher now, and if there was anyone up on top, they would see them.

Bear pushed the limits between speed and stealth.

Then they were on the other side. Dripping and cold, they pushed through the mud and into the forest.

After a quick count, and everyone accounted for, Bear turned them into the dark of the forest.

Not a word was spoken. They went as close to single file as possible, with Bear in the lead.

Up ahead fire twinkled and twisted through the trees. There were voices ahead, and Bear raised his fist.

He couldn't make out the words, but it sounded like two men talking. Guards, perhaps.

His sword whispered as he drew it from the sheath. Dozens more joined him.

9

Change in the Air

"What's this?" Sam looked down, his usual crate gone.

"Moved," Trent said, scooping out porridge from his bowl.

"Where?"

"To the castle," Ned said, shoving a spoon in the general direction. A line of workers trundled up and down the path.

They were pushing barrels, carrying goods, and had packed the carts with as much as they could.

"Inside?" Sam took his seat next to the others, digging in to the porridge. It was plain and needed something to spice it up. A pat of butter would have been nice.

"Orders from the duke. Secure everything, apparently." Kerien looked annoyed. "That's what I heard, at least."

"A precaution, nothing more," Ned said, lowering the tension that had suddenly built. The others seemed to relax, just a bit.

"Which means we won't be able to use the cart today either."

Sam stood back and thought about it. He had planned on bringing up a few beams that were ready, to get ahead of Bill and the masons.

One more day might not hurt, but if things changed then Bill might have another black mark to use against him.

"Looks like a good day to work in the workshop, then." Sam finished up his breakfast, listening to the conversation about the changes and answering at the appropriate points.

"Are they going to move us into the castle?" Trent asked, just as they were all finishing up.

Sam exchanged a glance with Ned. "I doubt it," Ned said. "Not enough room to fit us in there, and I don't suppose the Overseer would be too keen on having us right outside his window."

"No, I suppose not," Sam agreed. He rubbed his ribcage, still a bit tender. "Moving a hundred workers, not to mention their families, inside the walls would take an enormous amount of work." Not that the Overseer or the Duke would do any of it, or their contingent of a dozen or so guardsman stationed to protect them.

Mary stalked by with a countenance of storm clouds. Kerien didn't have the sense to leave her alone.

"Collecting dishes?" he asked, reaching out with his bowl.

She whirled, slapping it away. "Do I look like a maid to you?" Her voice was quiet, and dripping with venom. "Take it and wash it yourself." Kerien pulled back his hand fast, as if it had been bitten by a snake, a look of shock plastered across his face.

"I'm sorry," he managed to get out after a second. Mary glared at him a moment longer, then turned to the others. They backed up a step.

She walked off, grumbling under her breath. Sam caught a few words, some would make a sailor blush. The others were related to walking all the way up to the castle.

"What's gotten into her dress?" Kerien asked, when she was far out of earshot. His confidence had suddenly returned, and Sam had to hide a smile.

"They took the food, too. Now they'll have to bring it back down every night to cook. My guess is that the Overseer told them they couldn't stockpile anything out here." Sam turned and started walking up the path. "Are you coming? I have a feeling today is a good day to start moving supplies out of the workshop. If we're lucky, we'll get a day or two head start before we move everything."

The others caught up to him. "Where do you want to start?" Ned asked.

"The light stuff, tools first. Everything you can't bear parting with you can keep in the workshop, everything else goes into crates and barrels for the journey." The sun was up, but a cloudy sky blunted its rays. It was still humid enough for Sam to taste it and for his clothes to stick to his body.

"And there is a visitor. Wonder what he'll say?"

A guard was waiting in the lumber yard, itching the strap beneath his helmet.

"Morning," Sam said, walking up to him as the others filed into the workshop. "I'm assuming there's an order."

"From the Overseer," he said, nodding. Matthew, his name was Matthew. "You're to move all work inside the castle walls."

"Did he say where we're supposed to put it?"

"Not yet, that will be decided at a separate time."

"We need a dry place to keep everything."

Matthew looked into the workshop. "Don't you have a group of carpenters? I suggest you build one."

"Fair enough," Sam said, suppressing a spike of anger. "Will we get an extension on our castle work, then?"

"Nothing was said to me about it." Matthew furrowed his brow. "Anyway, I've given you your orders. That's all I was supposed to do."

"I understand. Thank you." Matthew walked off. Sam couldn't help but notice how loose the straps on his armor were. If there was a battle it would be easy to slide a knife, or a sword, right through his ribcage and into his heart.

But he wasn't running the guards and he couldn't tell him what to do. "I know you all heard that," Sam said, turning back to the workshop. They all pretended to be working, but the sudden interest in their tools didn't fool him. "Get out the crates."

Sam brushed off a fly, but it buzzed around his head, irritating him.

"They want us to move into the castle walls, that's what I heard," Trent said, leaning over the table and whispering to the group.

"You heard wrong," Kerien said, taking a bite out of his roll. He chewed with his mouth open, flecks of bread spewing as he talked. "There is no way the Overseer is going to let us into that place. Not in nine hells."

"Well, I heard it." Trent sat back, crossed his arms.

"You mean to tell me he's willing to take all of us in?" Kerien swept his hand around the Square. The tables were filled with masons, carpenters, smiths, and every other trade you could think of needed to build a castle. Not to mention their families running around and eating with them. "The unwashed masses?"

"Where would they put us?" Archie asked.

Kerien pointed to him, nodding. "He makes a good point."

"I dunno. We could build houses."

Kerien let out a laugh, loud enough to attract attention. Both Sam and Ned gave him a stern look. "They barely gave us the materials to build this place. You think they want us wasting time putting huts together when we're racing against time as it is? Not likely."

"Stranger things have happened," Ned said. He gummed his roll on the left side of his mouth, the side with his best teeth. Or what little teeth he had. "Strange feeling in my bones. I don't like it."

"You don't like anything, old man," Kerien said.

"Respect," Sam said.

"Sorry," Kerien mumbled. He didn't sound sincere.

"The Duke's brought changes to the castle, whether we like it or not," Archie said. His wife was working the bread line, still handing out food. She would join him soon, when she was done. "Some of those might be forced on the Overseer, too."

Changes. Changes like training workers in the art of combat. Or, in Sam's case, adding weight to his load each night, he refused. His shoulders ached, and the reminder made it worse. He rubbed them as he listened.

"We've had to move half the workshop up there without a good replacement to move it to." Kerien's brows were furrowed. "Now we have to work in the sun, with no protection from the heat."

"I could take you up to the tower with me. Trent could use some time dressing wood."

A ghastly look flashed across his face at the suggestion. "No, thanks." It almost made Sam laugh.

"Time to finish up. I've got work to do." Sam brushed off his hands, dumping the crumbs back onto his plate. At least they had plenty of bread and grain. Meat would be nice, though.

"We still have time," Kerien said.

"Take it. I'll be in the courtyard." Sam bid them goodbye and walked back alone. A shorter rest, but it would be worth it in the end.

Today was cooler, a sign of the change in seasons to come. Summer seemed to be giving way already to autumn, and a cloudless sky helped with the pleasant feeling he felt.

The quick walk back helped stretch his legs, and he went fast enough to shorten his breath.

Underneath the one lean-to they had been given was his project, nearly finished. A few late nights and time stolen as much as he could between jobs had gone a long way.

Now, it was nearly finished. The tree stretched out, splaying as large as he could make it. He was proud of this one, at the lifelike nature the trunk had taken on, and the detail of the leaves.

He sat and got to work, feeling the slope of the carving as he worked the gouge into the wood. The form was in there, hidden by the tree itself. All he had to do was let it out, little by little.

Carvings fell to the ground. He blew out the dust, wiping away the bigger chips, and focused on one leaf. It needed a more graceful curved, and he almost closed his eyes to do it.

There was a feeling in the wood that it enjoyed being worked under his hands. It was warm, and fine grained, seasoned enough to be hard, but not hard enough to blunt his blades.

He sat back, looking over his handiwork. *Better. Much better.*

The others had returned some time ago, and Trent was waiting at his side.

"How long have you been there?"

"A few minutes. How do you do that with the gouge, Master?"

Sam looked at the tool in his hands. Freshly oiled, recently sharpened. "A practiced hand. And a steady one. Ready?"

Trent nodded.

Sam made a final cut, brushed away, and set down his tool.

"Up to the top." Trent nodded, then they went to the unfinished tower.

The masons had worked past the beams already, laying the next course in a heaping hill that bunched to one side. They were working already, and gave them hard stares as they tapped out their stones and built them up.

With a nod, Sam greeted them, but they said nothing in return. The floorboard ledge was already in place, and with the beams set, they could start work on the structure to hold it in place.

They craned up smaller beams, laying them along the edge and cutting them to fit across the main beam. They rested on the ledge, which would be filled by the masons, and left about two feet in between each.

Sam decided to start on the south side and work up from there.

The first cross members were easy to put in place and cut, relatively small, and with the two of them manning the saw, it went fast. Scribing to fit was more difficult, but with a little chisel work it was manageable.

The feeling of eyes on him, however, was another matter. Every time he looked back at the masons one was staring at him. He thought about asking them why, but it wouldn't do any good.

The looks were affecting Trent. He was careless, preoccupied, and kept making mistakes. He dropped an offcut, even though his hand was beneath it, sending it tumbling into the tower below.

It hit with a clatter, and Trent winced. Sam gave him a stern look, but said nothing. All the masons looked at him then, with strange looks on their face.

A too deep cut from a chisel was the next thing. "What do we say?"

"A steady hand and a steady eye. First time."

"Then focus, the first time. Remember, you can't uncut." The lesson that he first learned, and learned with great embarrassment. An older apprentice to a hard man, his apprenticeship had been valuable beyond words.

"Yes, Master." Trent dropped his head but went back to his work, hand shaking.

"Everything else fades away. Everything else can wait. Guide your hand and be confident." Sam watched, partially shielding the boy with his body, straddled on the main beam.

The afternoon dragged on, but by the time dinner rolled around over half the cross members were laid and ready for the planking.

Sam stood, stretching his back and rubbing his neck. The masons had fled with the first sounds of the bell drifting up from below and had given them parting nasty glares. "A few more days and we'll be on to the next thing."

The next thing meant hours and hours more planking, dressing, and finishing timber for the floor. He wasn't relishing the thought, but a few more hours at his special project would help.

Sam gulped down dinner as fast as he could and went back to his carving. He managed to finish all but the border by the third bell, and after another punishment session with more water, went back.

The world slipped away as he worked, into the background. It was him and the wood, an image burned into it that had to get out.

At long last, in the wee hours of the night, he sat back and sighed.

It was done.

A few quick handfuls of sand to polish, and it gleamed bright and bold in the night. He couldn't wait until the morning to put it up, so he grabbed a hammer, and the custom nails delivered the day before and went into the castle.

It was quiet, and eerie. So full of the sounds of construction during the day, it echoed with the sound of his footsteps.

The night air had knocked down the smell of construction, leaving it fresh and woody smelling.

Sam knocked at the Duke's door, then pushed it aside.

After another trip for a ladder, and some wrestling, he had it in place. A few quick taps of the hammer on one side evened out his precarious position, and a minute later, it was in place.

He stepped back and admired his work.

It wasn't the best carving in the world, but it was his best. It was imposing, large, grand, and would satisfy the purpose for what he built.

Of that, he was sure.

Let it be a surprise. Sam yawned, gather his tools, and shut the door quietly as he left.

It had been a long day, but it was well worth it. He hoped this effort would secure what he needed most right now.

An ally.

10

INTERRUPTED

The scream woke him up. Sam's eyes flashed open. The night was cool, the smell like normal, but there was something wrong.

A gurgle of death brought him fully out of sleep.

He sprung to his feet, struggled to put on his boots, and rushed out of the hut.

Blood pumping, Sam turned left and right to see what the problem was.

"Raiders, raiders!" Someone was yelling something from the forest.

He didn't hesitate.

Sam turned and ran, ringing the alarm bell in the Square. If it was a false alarm, he would have to deal with it.

The bell was loud and left his ears ringing.

Workers started to assemble, and their families, asking what was going on.

"I don't know, get to the castle."

Sam looked into the forest, trying to see what was out there. It was dark, and still.

Not even a night bird calling.

The hairs on the back of his neck rose, and he unconsciously clutched at his side.

But there was nothing there. Of course.

He relaxed his hand, stretched it out, and took a deep breath. About half the workers were up or on the road already. Bleary eyes looked at him, children cried.

And guards were coming the other direction. "What is the meaning of this?" One asked. He had a smashed nose and a glare in his eyes. Dawain, Sam thought. Matthew was the other.

"A scream, to the south. An alarm." Sam didn't keep looking at him, but turned his attention back to the forest. "Something is wrong."

"You've woken everyone up, that's what's wrong," Dawain said, irritated. "And you disturbed our watch. If we have to come down every time one of you gets too twitchy, we'll never get anything done."

A movement. Sam snapped his head in that direction. There it was again. Something was moving.

"Get down." Sam dropped, an unusual sound tickling his ears.

"Get — " An arrow struck Dawain, brushing above Sam. He clutched at it and cried out.

"Attack!" Matthew drew his sword. Dawain stumbled and turned, and another arrow hit him in the back.

The gates were a few hundred yards away. "There are too many," Sam said. "We've got to get back to the castle." The stream of workers and families had slowed to a trickle, but they were running now. "Come on."

"Go, I'll stop them." Matthew advanced into the night.

Sam shook his head, then ducked as another arrow flew by. That was aimed at his head. "Come on."

He pulled Dawain over his shoulder. The man was in shock, mumbling something over and over again.

He could still walk, though, and Sam led him up the path. He glanced back.

Fighters were pouring out of the woods, less than two hundred yards away from the makeshift worker's village.

They looked angry. And large. And all of them were bearing deadly looking weapons.

The other guard had seen them too and was sprinting in their direction. Sam pushed harder, breaking them both into a run. The dust of the path got in his eyes and mouth, tasting like dry sand.

He spit it out and kept running.

Ahead of him the screams had started, of pure terror. The iron gate was creaking, breaking free of its position. It had been closed before, when it was installed and tested, but had lain open since.

It looked like they wouldn't have much time until it was shut.

Arrows flew by him now, and he zigzagged left and right as much as he could to try and avoid them, making them as much of a difficult target to hit as possible. It worked, and Matthew caught up to them.

He didn't stop, but ran past. Sam wanted to cry out, but fueled his surprise into his legs, carrying on the wounded man despite the lack of help.

A quick glance told him why the man had run past. Dozens of fighters had flooded the streets of the worker's makeshift town, now all converging on the path up to the castle.

And even worse, there was a party of them rushing the gate along the edge of the wall. "By the wall," Sam cried out. He wished he could point, he wished he had both hands free to signal, but Dawain groaned, reminding him that his life was in his hands.

They weren't moving fast, though, and they still had at least a hundred yards to go.

The workers had made it, all shuffling into the relative protection of the gates, and were milling about the courtyard beyond.

Clanking from the gates, black and shining in the moonlight, called out to him, urged him on.

Finally, someone on the castle walls had seen the other raiders and were firing arrows at them. It didn't stop them, if they could get inside before the gates closed, the defenders would have no chance. This had to be their aim.

Sam's legs were like lead now, weighed down by the full weight of Dawain. Their lead was shrinking even now, and cries of war struck up from the raiders.

They knew they would catch them.

He dug deep inside, finding the part of him he thought best left alone, and touched it. Just enough to raise his strength, just enough to keep him going.

The anger and energy helped, and he sped up. He took the other man's arms on his shoulders and hefted him onto his back, feet dragging behind.

The shift in weight helped, putting his effort into muscles unused in the chase, and Sam ran for all he was worth.

His heart pounded, his lungs burned, and the gate came down.

Now it was halfway closed. The raiders were less than a hundred yards away, sprinting along the wall for cover.

A quarter left. The war cries were closer.

He dare not look behind.

His mouth was dry but tasted like iron, his nose strained with the breath in his body.

A few more yards. What felt like hands reached out behind him, spurring him on to sprint.

He ducked, clearing the gate just in time, and fell forward. Dawain sprawled into the dust.

There were hands clutching him, pulling him.

The gate slammed shut behind him, its iron bands enveloping his hurt and aching body.

Sam fell to his knees, and they pulled him forward. The air tasted sweet, cool in his mouth. Someone forced water into his hands, and he drank of the coolness.

It went down into his belly, a big slug of cold that shivered through his stomach and out to the rest of his body, cooling him.

"Well done," the crowd said. Hands were clapping his back, but he was short of breath and dizzy.

The guards were running through the yard in an uneasy state of alarm. Half were dressed, while others were still in nightclothes, and Captain Yand strode through them, shouting and ordering them to their posts.

"Look after him," Sam said. They rushed Dawain away, careful of the arrows sticking out of his back and front. He was still awake and alive, but the whites of his eyes showed as they rolled back into his head.

Confusion reigned in the courtyard. The night's stillness shattered, broken like pottery on a rock, and voices were talking, shouting, screaming.

Sam tried to stay on his feet, but his legs gave out and he sat down hard. The ground met him, hard as rock.

"Sam, talk to me." Ned was there, at his side, worried eyes covered in bushy brows that were pulled down tight. His arms were on Sam's shoulders, shaking him slightly.

"Fine. I'm fine." There was banging from the gate, the sound of metal on metal.

The taste of iron was in his mouth, and he spit it out. Blood. *Must have cut my lip.*

"They came out of nowhere," Archie said, clutching his wife. Sandra looked wild, her eyes as big as saucers.

"They came from the forest. Probably came across the river when no one was looking." Sam regained his breath, words no longer labored. "They were here without warning."

He could see them gathered at the gate. Sam wished they would shut the big, wooden doors that had taken so long to make, but no one had had the sense to do it.

Captain Yand was directing archers to the front to shoot in between the openings in the iron. "Get out of the way, go somewhere else, behind the gate," he bellowed.

The workers and their families were happy to oblige, and in the scuffle and rush, some semblance of order returned.

They picked up who they had to and moved out of the line of sight. Sam saw a dozen guards.

That was it.

That was all the fighting men they had. To hold this castle from dozens of hardened fighters. He caught glimpses of their faces.

Scars crossed their bodies. Their armor was cut and torn, battered in battles long ago. These were no mere raiders, they were organized.

"You see it too, don't you?" Sam asked, helped along by Ned.

"I do. Evil times have befallen us." They shuffled forward, joining the others safely out of the way of returned arrow fire. "I prayed this day would never come, but now it has."

Stars twinkled above, oblivious to their plight. What had once been filled with the smell of dust and rock, progress on a fortress to stand against attack, had turned to the smell of blood and battle.

"They found out, and sent a force to capture it before it was too late," Sam said, taking a seat and leaning against the hard stones of the keep.

Ned gave him a halfhearted smile. "Too late for them, it seems."

"Well, now we fight back, then wait for them to go." Something orange and yellow was glowing, flickering light through the night.

"What is that?" someone asked farther away.

Sam knew. He smelled the smoke, even from here.

"Fire!" someone else shouted. "The village is on fire!"

His clothes, his bed. The small place he could call his own. It was gone now.

And the rest of the wood would be burned too. All that effort, all that time.

The beams, the timbers.

Oak, ash, cherry. It had taken months to season some of the wood, and now it would be gone, burned to ash.

Sam clenched his hand, drawing it around a clump of dust. He squeezed with all his might, breathing deep to counteract his anger. The sand was hard, bit into his hand.

He didn't care. He kept squeezing until he couldn't bear it anymore. Until that red of anger receded. That thing that resided deep inside him had to stay asleep.

"Trent," Sam said. The young man, eyes wide from the excitement of the night, was at his side in a flash. "Go see if you can tell if they destroyed the workshop."

With a nod, he was off, running to get a better view. He chose the wall, running up the rough steps that ascended to the heights above.

"Why did you send him?" Ned asked.

"I need to know."

"You could have sent anyone else."

"I could have."

Ned stared at him. "Why?"

"He loved that workshop. It was the only one he's ever known." Sam looked down, dropping the sand back to the earth. "He needs to know it's gone. Forever. Needs to see it with his own eyes."

Now that the shock had worn off, the others were stirring. Curiosity had taken some, and they had peeked out from behind the keep wall to see.

Yand was still yelling orders, directing men to and fro. A few yells, a few more curses. Some in a tongue that he wasn't familiar with.

The Belmarchers. Why had they chosen now to attack, after all this time?

They must have been watching them, marking their progress. Any earlier and they would have walked into the castle through the unfinished gate, or the holes in the castle walls.

Perhaps finishing the gate had helped. He looked up at the half finished stone tower. Its top looked like a toothy grin against the night sky, like it had taken half a bite out of it.

That tower would do no good now. The warning was gone and over with.

Sam shivered. The cool air of the night had sapped some of his strength, but the few minutes of rest had helped with everything else. He didn't want to believe it, wished it were untrue. It kept calling to him.

He stood, surprising Ned and the other carpenters who had gathered around. "Where are you going?"

Starting for the tower, he looked back for a moment. "I'm going to see for myself."

11

BURNED

Sam met Trent on the stairs.

"It's burned." Tears streaked down the man's face, tracking through the dust and the ash. Big plumes of smoke were roiling up in the air behind him.

What a fire it would make.

"Go back to the others, get some rest." This was going to be a long night. Sam knew Trent wouldn't be able to sleep. None would, after what had happened.

Still, it was the best he could do. "Why did they have to do it?" Trent asked. Fire raged in his eyes.

The same fire Sam felt in his heart.

"Like any other reason a man does what is evil. Because they wanted to."

Trent looked like he had something else to say, but held his tongue and rushed by Sam on the narrow staircase.

He moved to let the boy pass and continued the long climb to the top. When he got there, he stopped dead in his tracks.

The fires blazed in the makeshift village, the thatched roofs of the hastily constructed shacks lit up and licked by great tongues of fire.

He felt the heat even from the top of the wall and saw its distortions as it wavered and flew into the sky. The workshop was on fire, bodies stuffing burning torches into the wood piles.

They crackled and spit as they burned the fresh wood. All the potential in them was licked away, consumed by flames.

An arrow flew by his head, and Sam ducked back down behind the wall. The fighters were still out there, ready to kill them all.

He had a feeling that if they got in, they would spare no one. They were the advanced party, small but light. Able to move quickly, unburdened by the long chain of supplies an army needed.

Which meant more were coming.

Sam took a deep breath, the fires of rage threatening to burn him away. He had come to this place to escape war, not to be in the thick of it.

Soldiers yelled down below, clashing with each other over the gate. Someone finally gave the order to shut the wood gates, and they were creaking closed.

Still, the fighting went on. Sam risked another look, searching for the archers. They had taken up residence to the left of the village and were peppering the wall with arrows. One saw him and raised a bow, but Sam dropped down out of sight.

He had managed to count them. At least a dozen archers that he could see, and presumably a larger number of fighters at the gate.

They would need to get in. The gate was the weak point, but defenses more than made up for it. Even now he expected they had stoked the fires in the room above the murder holes, ready to drop down burning pitch and oil on the attackers.

But that would only deter them, not keep them away.

Sam felt the cool of the stone against the back of his head, sucking the heat from his head. Smoke hung thick in the air now, on the cloudless, calm night. So thick he could taste it in his mouth and feel it on his tongue. It was oily and bitter.

The others were huddled in a mass next to the keep. The Overseer was out now, dressed and perplexed, walking next to the duke, who looked angry.

One guardsman rushed up to the workers, calling for their help. Sam roused himself and rushed down the stairs, joining a reluctant group of the strongest workers to follow.

The doors were still open, cracked down the middle. Six men were trying to push each side shut, including Captain Yand, but hands and weapons of the attackers held them back.

Arrows flew into the castle from the opening, and the guardsmen urged them in. "Either side now, push for all your worth. Your lives depend on it."

"Put your backs into it," Yand growled. Sam found a spot on the far side, a quick sprint across the opening before any arrows could hit him, and shoved into the wood with his shoulder.

The locking beam was ready, but it was too far open to put it into the iron braces that held it.

Sam dug in, lowering his shoulder and finding his footing. He pushed against the dirt, which gave way a little, and tried again.

"Push, push!" They pushed and strained. The doors closed an inch. Someone on the other side cried out as something snapped. A hand, a weapon, Sam couldn't tell.

He kept pushing, as did the others. Inch by inch, it closed. The opening at the middle narrowed.

"Get the lock!" Yand bellowed. A few men broke off and picked up the thick, stout beam that would lock into place, lifting it over the heads of the pushers.

But their momentary abandonment of the doors allowed the enemy to push it back open, an inch at least.

Arrows flew through the opening, one hitting a man in the arm. He cried out.

Sam pushed, trying to get traction. The locking bar was in one set of braces, but the doors were too much to put it in the other set.

Men gasped around him, groaned, and grunted. The smell of blood and sweat mingled with smoke from the fires. Sam gritted his teeth and pushed for all he was worth.

"Put your backs into it," Yand was on the other side of the doors. Veins stuck out on his forehead, and his face was red.

Something snapped, and the door shut to his left. Sam felt his side give, then it, too, slammed shut.

Hands scrambled, fingers grasped. His own found the wood and pulled down. The locking bar slid into place.

Sam slid down against the door, gasping for breath. Men leaned against the wood nursing wounds or trying to recover their strength.

Yand was breathing hard, but stumbled back, drawing his sword. "To the walls. There's no time to rest." He pulled a guardsman off the door, who stumbled and staggered to the stairs. The others caught the hint and streamed up to the wall.

Only a few men were left at the doors, Sam and a few masons. The enemy forces were yelling and pounding on the door, shudders running into his body.

Sam stepped back. His shoulder hurt from where he had jammed it into the wood, and he rubbed feeling back into it.

"What are we going to do?" a guard asked.

"Keep calm. We have a thick wall between us and them." Sam looked up at it, newly finished. He shuddered to think what would have happened had they come just a few months earlier, when it was still open.

But then, he knew what would have happened.

There would have been no one to dig their graves.

"How can you be so calm?" The man's hands shook. Damien, Sam recalled. "They burned our homes..."

Sam thought about it for a moment. Yes, it was difficult, terrorizing, unthinkable. But it had happened. "I don't know, but I'm too tired to be upset."

It was true, with so little sleep, his body felt exhausted. He needed a break.

The shouts and screams would keep him up. The excitement from the night was too much. On the other side, the sound of splashing water, then cries of pain. They had done it. Sam imagined they would retreat now, far back out of arrow range, and leave them alone.

"Go back to the others, get some rest." Sam turned to go back up the wall, taking the stairs carefully in his exhaustion.

He wouldn't be able to last much longer. A quick glance back showed that the workers and their families were being herded inside the keep. Sam wondered where they were going to put them. The main room? On the finished side wings?

He reached the top, turning the thought out of his mind, and joined the others at the edge.

They were retreating, pulling back through the side of the village, which had burned through most of the shacks and was now a smoldering, festering ruin.

Twangs from the bows of the defenders were few and far between, despite Yand's urging. The enemy bowmen had fallen back too, joining the band of warriors as they set up a distance away.

The retreat was orderly, and they even carried their wounded out with them. These men were disciplined, hardened by battle.

The chances of them simply giving up and going home despite the loss of the element of surprise was going to be low.

"What are you doing up here?" Yand demanded.

"Checking the village, sir," Sam said, turning to face him. The man looked awful, covered in dirt, mud, and blood mixed with ash. Sam wondered if he didn't look the same. The face he wore was one of anger.

"Get down below with the others. This place is for fighters only." There was no room for negotiation in his tone.

So, Sam bowed and walked down the stairs. The smell of smoke was clearing, now just a hint on the fresh night air, but the sounds of panic and terror from the families continued.

He joined them, entering into the great hall that had been finished for some time. It was barren, still waiting on his carpenters to furnish, and was another thing on the list that needed to be done.

Sam almost laughed at the thought. That was gone now. What would his priorities be? To build more doors so that the enemy couldn't come in?

He found the other carpenters huddled near the front. Children were crying, women were trying to calm them, and the men reached out to him with questions as soon as they saw him.

"The gates are shut," he said, raising his hands to quiet them. They rushed around him, peppering him with more questions so that he couldn't even respond. "Where is the Overseer?"

"With the Duke," someone said. Sam furrowed his brow.

"We're safe for now." A great sigh of relief seemed to ripple through them. "Has there been any direction?"

"No, we came in here to get out of the way and be some-where safe," David said.

"Where are we supposed to sleep? The children are tired." Mary clutched at her two boys. Their eyes were red, and they held onto her legs for dear life.

Sam felt it too. He looked around. There was plenty of space for every family if they spread out. Everyone was looking to him, even Bill cast a watchful eye his way.

"We'll sleep here, behind the walls of the keep. That will put more than a few inches of stone between us and whatever else is out there. Spread out, let every man and family have his share."

They pushed to the back of the room, as far away from the entrance doors as they could. Sam didn't mind and looked out over everyone, making sure it was as orderly as possible.

They divided up by trade, like they always had at meals. The masons and their families, the largest group, took the farthest back. The smiths were next, then the carpenters, and everyone else.

Sam took the spot as close to the door as he could. There was no bedding to speak of, but the children were laying heads on their mother and father.

A hush fell over the room. Outside was quiet, punctuated only by a shouted order here or there. Somewhere an owl hooted, a strange reminder of the natural world that still existed.

He sat down, leaning against the stone wall. Anxious eyes looked out, but the excitement of the night quickly faded away. One by one, they went to sleep.

Sam felt himself drifting off, but still they were all looking to him. he wasn't sure what he could do for them.

He wouldn't fight, and he couldn't save them. They were trapped here, as much as the enemy was kept out, they were kept in.

Not knowing what tomorrow would bring, Sam let himself be overtaken by exhaustion and slipped into a blissfully empty sleep.

12

SECURE

Dawn brought a new day and a painful rousing. His body ached from the strain of the previous day and the rough sleeping conditions.

Dozens of families were strewn about the great hall, and sunlight streamed in from the openings near the top of the ceiling.

Dust motes played in the shafts of light, drifting in the otherwise quiet room. Light snores and heavy breathing were the only sounds.

Sam got up and stretched. A few others were awake, but the vast majority were still asleep. The guards were nowhere to be seen.

He went outside, still groggy from the sleep, but waking with the rest of the world. The sun rose empty, no sunrise to speak of, in a clear sky. Smoke still drifted up from the direction of the village, white wisps that curled up into the air and were taken away by a gentle, rising wind.

Men were on the wall standing guard, two on each wall. The rest were nowhere to be seen. Sam took care of his business in the corner, then walked back over dusty ground to the gate.

From this side the wood looked fine. The locking bar was still in place and seated in its braces. Other than the dust and

89

mud kicked up in the hasty shutting, it bore no evidence of ill use.

He wondered if they would care if he went up to the wall. He longed to look out, see what the enemy was doing. Were they encamped, or had they retreated in failure?

Judging from the hard stares of the sentries, who looked even more exhausted than he felt, it was the former.

Eventually, he decided to risk it, and climbed to the top.

"You shouldn't be here," the guard said. It was Matthew, and his heart didn't seem in it.

"I'll be gone in a moment, just wanted to take a look." Matthew glanced back uneasily, but the keep was silent and there was no sight of the Overseer or of Captain Yand.

"Make it quick."

He was right, they had made camp. A fire ringed by tents was far off in the distance, well out of bow-shot or even sortie range.

It was haphazard, but not undisciplined. The tents were tied down and staked into the ground.

He wondered how long it would take for them to come back. One of the enemy soldiers was tending the fire, adding logs every so often to keep it going.

"Thank you," Matthew said roughly.

"For what?"

"Last night. You carried Dawain. I should have done that."

"You raised the alarm, allowed us to shut the gate in time. I'd say you proved yourself well."

Matthew turned away. "It sounds like he might make it."

"I'm glad of it."

"You should go now. You've been here too long." His eyes searched the horizon, ignoring Sam.

Seeing all he needed to, Sam acquiesced. The wind was picking up, and the sun was getting higher. His legs felt like jelly on the way down, a combination of tiredness and the unsettling oneness of the stairs.

At the bottom, he wondered what to do. Construction would halt, of that he was certain, but what else would they be tasked with?

The others were waking up now, coming out in a long stream to relieve themselves in the corner of the yard. Sam mentally went over the inventory of wood in his head.

There wasn't enough to build housing for everyone, not even for tents. Where would they all stay?

He put the thought out of his mind. That was for the Duke and the Overseer to decide. Not him.

"What are we going to do about it?" Duke Hornblood sat in his chair, eyes bloodshot.

"We need reinforcement, Sir," Overseer Rhys said. "We should send for them as soon as possible."

"They have us trapped in here. I have to agree." Captain Yand stood next to the Overseer in front of the desk. His eyes briefly flickered to the crest above the Duke, then back to their steely gaze.

"And this is the advance party?"

"That's what I think," Yand said. He stood with his hands behind his back at forty-five degrees, legs spread exactly shoulder width. Despite the mess on his uniform, he could have been on the parade ground.

"Then we send a messenger, go to my father or the King." The Duke stood up, paced furiously behind his desk. "They'll come with armies and fight back the incursion. They have to."

"Well..." The Overseer shifted his weight. His belly jiggled as he did. His mouth twisted.

"Out with it." The Duke turned on him.

"With the invasion to the east, the King might not have much to send." He hastily continued under the impetuous gaze. "At least until later in the year, after the fighting season is over."

"That assumes they can get here," Yand said. "The passes might be blocked."

"Even with a message we might not see help until when, next year?"

"In the worst case, I'm afraid so." The Overseer flinched as he spoke, expecting the worst.

The Duke stopped pacing and drew in a deep breath. "I was afraid of something like this. We don't have the men or material to break out, do we?"

"Not without significant losses. Even then, we're over-manned." Yand tilted his head down. "Permission to speak openly, sir?"

"Granted." The Duke took his chair again, tapping his foot against the floor.

"We should expect attacks. Often. They'll probe our weaknesses, try and find a way in. They'll add men to their ranks, grow their raiding party into a small army if they can. This was supposed to be a surprise attack. Now that they've failed, we can expect them to come hard and come often until we...dissuade them."

"So, how do we survive?"

"Fight them off. We have supplies, arrows, and food to last. We'll repel anything they decide to throw at us."

"For how long?" the Duke asked.

Yand was silent, but shifted, showing his first real hint of discomfort. "We will have to do an inventory of everything inside the castle. Luckily, due to your grace's foresight and diligence," at that he gave a small bow. Of course, it was his idea. "We brought in as much as we could before the attack. A mere trifle remained outside the castle walls."

"We're stuck here with them?" The Overseer recoiled, the thought just striking him. "Oh, dear..."

The Duke took a sip of his now warm wine. "Whatever do you mean, dear Overseer?" He gave him a nasty smile, and the Overseer paled.

"Nothing," he said, gulping. "I will organize the inventory and come back with my report when it is complete."

"Do that." The Duke stood and stretched, taking a glance back at his crest. It had appeared there quite unexpectedly, if not welcome. He felt better sitting with it hanging above him. It reminded any with him of the magnitude of who they were speaking to.

But, at the same time, it was a constant reminder of the weight of duty and horror that hung above. All things considered, the good outweighed the bad.

He would have to thank that carpenter, it was well made and stout. "Is there anything else we need to discuss?" He yawned. It had been hours since he had any real sleep to speak of.

"I've set up rotating shifts of guard work. They'll raise the alarm if anything happens with our new...friends."

Duke Hornblood nodded. "Good. Dismissed."

Captain Yand snapped to attention. The Duke almost heard the crack through the air as he moved and saluted. With a quick face, he turned right and marched out of the room.

Always a stickler for decorum and ceremony.

"Good day, your excellency." The Overseer bowed, his eyes sunken. He looked just as tired as the Duke felt.

The Duke let them go, then went to the small window that overlooked the castle courtyard below. Men and women were milling about, uncertainty in their faces and their movements.

A great weight had been laid on him, but he never imagined he would be in this situation.

"Trial by fire indeed, Uncle," he said to himself, watching his vassals work.

"Over here." The Overseer's voice drifted from the Keep. Sam turned to watch. He was alone, no guard to speak of.

His guards must be occupied on the walls.

The workers turned to watch, and the Overseer beckoned them in.

They milled about at first, but the look of frustration on the Overseer's face brought them in.

The sun was high in the sky now, almost to noon, and they had spent an unproductive morning talking and wandering around. Sam made sure to keep the carpenters working, setting up a temporary workshop, and they were working on the frame for a more permanent home before the meal bell had rung.

The Overseer wiped the sweat from his brow, the sun shining in a cloudless sky.

Sam wondered what the attackers were doing. Why had they pulled back so? Did they not sense they could overwhelm them?

He glanced back to the gate, strong and heavy. The walls had been designed well, sloped gently to allow a full range of attack from anyone above, with no place to hide, and crenelations for the archers to take cover between shots. They must have thought it wasn't worth the risk, and the boiling liquids being dropped on them, to try it again.

Smoke rose from the gatehouse. There would be a fire kept up, and boiling water or oil always at the ready to be dropped down on the attackers stupid enough to get too close.

If he were on the other side he would be making a ram right now, or ladders to scale the wall in the night.

The Overseer's voice brought his attention again.

"Divide up into your prospective trades and take stock of everything we have. Masons, you're in charge of cataloging the foodstuffs, carpenters, the bedding and housing supplies, and everyone else can pitch in where needed."

"What's going to happen?" Someone called out. "We've been here all day with no news."

Others voiced their agreement, causing the Overseer's mouth to twitch. He held up his hands.

"We've been attacked, as you know, by Belmarch raiders. They've taken up camp just outside of range of our arrows."

"What are you going to do about it?" Someone said.

A flash of irritation passed across the big man's face. "They will be dealt with in time. The King's forces will come to save us. We're going to send a messenger to hurry them along, but in the meantime we have some work to do."

"Work? What work?" Bill asked. "We can't get to the quarry to cut stone, so we can't build the walls. We're stuck here with nothing to do and a whole lot of nothing to do it with." His masons agreed.

"Take care," the Overseer said, drawing himself up to his full height. His booming voice rang out in the courtyard. "I still oversee this castle until it is finished. The Duke would not react kindly to those who step out of place in questioning me."

Bill backed down, and his masons grumbled. They outnumbered the carpenters four to one and made up the majority of the workers. With the amount of stone going into the walls, it made sense, but Sam was starting to feel uneasy about it.

Although, now that he thought about it, he wouldn't have to worry about the schedule as much anymore.

Wind kicked up the dust, spraying it into everyone's face, then died down again. Sam spit the gritty dirt out of his mouth and wiped it from his eye. It scratched against his eyelid as he did.

It seemed to dampen the mood on the crowd, and the Overseer glared at them. Hearing more no objections, he said, "Get to work."

Stalking off, the Overseer retreated to the safety of the keep, and the coolness of its walls.

The group split into the respective trades, and the carpenters gathered around Sam. He kept an eye on the masons as they milled around Bill.

"Trent, go back to the supplies and pick up anything valuable you can. The best chisels, planes, and saws. Take it to the keep and lock it into the empty room on the second floor." Sam slipped him a key.

Trent looked down, surprised, then back up. "Why is that?"

"I'm afraid things are about to get ugly."

13

ALL DAY AND NOTHING TO DO

Trent rushed off as fast as Sam had ever seen him go.

"What are you thinking?" Ned asked quietly.

"I'm thinking now is a...volatile time. We've been surrounded by enemies, people are scared, and things happen that might not work out for the best," Sam said. He kept his eyes on his carpenters, but watched everyone else out of the side of his peripheral vision.

Volatile was putting it nicely, this was a recipe for disaster. Idle hands, and a few hours of discussion turning them into a united force.

The question would be, is it a force that would preserve life, or take it?

"In the meantime, we'll do what the Overseer asks. Ned, take Archie with you to inventory the lumber. I'll take Kerien to check on the tools. If we have any luck, Trent will have slipped into the keep by then and we'll have a stash for ourselves."

They worked out the finer details, agreed to meet back near the keep after dinner, and dispersed.

Ned and Archie went to the stacks of lumber, staged for the beams and supports that would have been needed for the rest of the keep. Sam looked up at the tower. He wasn't sure they would ever finish it now.

Kerien, for once, looked nervous. "Bill sounded angry."

"Wouldn't you, if your supply of ale dried up, stuck in a burning village?" Sam strode away, and Kerien ran to catch up. "Men will do strange things for alcohol. Desperate things."

"You don't think they'd — " Kerien swallowed hard, "do something rash, do you?"

"We're stuck in a castle with few defenders and even less competent ones. They sent us the guards who couldn't be trusted anywhere else, disposable, unusable. Captain Yand is the only soldier in this place." *Well, except one other.*

"But they know how to fight."

"Not like the Belmarch raiders do. They'd tear them to pieces in an instant, and spit on their graves afterward." Sam thought a moment. "I think they'll send for help, if they can. A rider, probably, if they had any horses. Of course, since we don't have horses the river would be the next best thing."

"We don't have any boats."

"That might be a problem." They had reached the makeshift workshop. Trent was stuffing supplies into a large crate. "Make sure you take the back way and be sure to be quiet. I don't want anybody seeing you take those in."

"I think I have everything." Trent looked around hastily. Sam peered into the crate, moved a few things around. He'd done well, got most of what Sam was thinking.

"Good," Sam said. "Go." He clapped him on the back. Trent nodded, collected the crate, and took off.

The boy knew how to move, and move quietly, when he wanted. He was always sneaking up behind Sam when he least expected him.

"We'll start at the front and work our way back. You start counting and I'll tally."

"Saws first?" Kerien held up a two-handed saw.

Sam nodded.

The inventory took longer than he expected. They had managed to get more out than he realized. There was enough left to stock the workshop with everything they needed, with the set that Trent had taken with him.

He showed up a few minutes later than Sam expected him, but gave a good report. Everything was locked away and safe.

Evening was coming, the sun halfway down the sky, and the smell of burning ash had finally fallen away from the wind. There was a fire burning in the courtyard, and food cooking over it. Soup, from the smell of it.

They finished everything and went to join the others milling around the campfire. Sam stopped at the well, took up a bucket, and splashed his face.

It was cool and felt good. The dust from the day washed away, and he used the rest of the water in the bucket to wash off his hands.

Bill was standing off to the side, surrounded by his crew. Sobriety had not done him well. Large, black bags highlighted the bloodshot eyes.

They met his, and Sam saw the danger in them.

It made him angry and flared up his rage. After all of this, after the attack, and this man still had a grudge against him.

What have I done to him, other than help him? Sam remembered being overly helpful in accommodating their schedule, trying to get his work ready a day or two before theirs. In turn, they changed what they were doing. He now realized it was on purpose.

His hands dug into the bucket. It was hard, solid wood and damp from use in the well. He wanted to throw it at Bill, chuck it against his head.

But that would accomplish nothing. Sam took a deep breath, letting the smell of dinner fill his lungs. Bill had pushed his way to the front of the line and was ladling out his portion.

Sam dropped the bucket back into place, letting it clang against the stone wall of the well, and returned to join the others at the back of the line.

Ned and Archie came up. "How did it go?"

Ned gave him a side look. "Better than yours, apparently."

Sam tried to relax more, let his scowl drop. "Sorry, not your fault."

"Whatever it is, I'd stay away from you right now."

"How are the supplies?"

Archie scratched the back of his head. "Plenty of oak," he said. "In various sizes and lengths." That was to be expected, as it was the main timber in the area. "A bit of other wood, but I'm sure there won't be enough to continue outfitting the keep with furniture."

"I thought we should have brought the rest up here," Kerien said.

"You said no such thing." Archie's eyes narrowed as they rested on the younger man. "Don't be making up stories."

Chastened, Kerien glowered at Archie. He was a bigger man, and would put up with no sass. "Any word on the attackers?" Ned asked, trying to change the subject.

"Nothing," Sam said, and the others agreed.

"I heard they've set up camp in the village," the man in front of them said, turning their way. His name was Dave, a farmer. "Tore up the fields too. I hope they go home soon."

"Not likely," Ned said. "They're like wolves. Once they've tasted the blood, it would take killing them to get off the scent again. I've heard it before."

"Then there's no hope for us, is there?" Trent asked. He looked forlorn, beaten down by the circumstances. It was the most dejected Sam had ever seen him.

"Look here, don't you think about despairing now." Sam pointed to the walls. "We've got a few feet of good, solid rock between us and them. It'll take more than a few arrows to break our resolve."

But there were some things that could. Walls could come down faster than they go up, given the right persuasion. There was no need to tell Trent that, though.

"We learned to fight and I didn't even get a chance," Trent said. Sam bit back a laugh. The boy might be a promising carpenter, but his martial skills had left much to be desired.

Taking to the plane was a whole lot different than taking to a sword.

What am I thinking? Sam turned back to Dave. "Any word on how many, or if they came alone?"

"I heard there are dozens, if not hundreds, of them. They've hidden more in the trees to try and fool us, to lure us out of the castle." He got to the front of the line and held out a bowl to be filled. "They just wait for us to lower our guard and they'll strike, you'll see."

He probably wasn't too far off the mark, but Sam doubted they had an extra stash of warriors hidden somewhere. Why they wouldn't use them to attack and overwhelm them at the outset was a silly prospect.

However, he had underestimated enemies before. An old scar reminded him of a time.

"Are you telling stories again, Dave?" Martha dipped into the big pot, stirred it around and pulled out a spoonful to dump in his bowl. It steamed from the heat, and a few potatoes slipped inside. "Shame on you."

"I swear I saw them in the woods. Mark my words." He pointed his spoon at her and closed one eye.

"Go along then." She clicked her tongue. "Next."

Trent went first, then Kerien. She gave them the same amount.

"Can I get more than that?" Kerien asked, staring into the bowl. It wasn't filled.

She gave him a long stare and put a hand on her hip. "No. We've decided to ration the food until we know how long it will take to get supplies back in the castle. I'll have no grumbling either."

Kerien said something under his breath, but then smiled and moved along. When everyone else had gotten their food, Sam let his be filled and joined them on makeshift log benches near the outskirts of the fire.

The heat of the day had died, and it was cooler than the day before. Sam stirred his weak broth, searching for a clump of something more substantial. He found it and chewed, the taste of potato exploding with the soft piece.

"We're in here and they're out there," Archie said, staring out over the gate. "I can't believe it. It happened so fast."

"That it did, lad," Ned said mournfully. "Sometimes that's how life goes. Up and out in the sunshine one day and a squall the next."

"We should do something about it then," Kerien said, glowering. He hadn't spoken since his reprimand, and Sam could tell it was behind his eyes simmering. "Why don't we catch them by surprise?"

"Because we're a bunch of tradesmen, not soldiers. That's why." Sam drank a spoonful of the broth after he spoke. It was still good, salty, with a hint of spice.

"We've been training," Kerien said, straightening. "We could fight them if they gave us weapons."

Sam glanced in Bill's direction. One of his masons handed him another bowl, and he took it greedily. It was filled to the brim. Behind him the door to the keep opened, letting out a serious-looking Captain Yand. "Careful what you wish for, Kerien."

"On your feet," the head guard bellowed. Sam stood, and others scrambled. In a few seconds everyone was standing.

Yand strode forward, flanked by guards on either side and the Overseer on his right. "Good evening." His voice held an edge of steel. "I've heard you all have been asking about ou r...situation. Let me assure you we have planned for this very eventuality." He smiled, showing off a row of gleaming teeth. "And these preparations that you found so odious before will allow us to hold out against a bloodthirsty and determined enemy.

"It is true that these are Belmarch, but they are no simple raiders. They bear the standard of the Raltone's." Murmurs ran through the crowd. "I see you've heard of him."

Sam hadn't, and looked around. Some people had gone pale, and there were a few trembling.

"The advantage we used to have, mainly that the Belmarch are a bloodthirsty and strife-driven people, has become quite tenuous. They are, for the moment united, most against their will, and if this unification is completed, shall be a force to reckon with."

"This was an ad hoc attack, carried out before preparations were complete, hoping to surprise us and loose us from the foothold we have in the castle before it was complete.

"Luckily for us, they were too late. Overseer Rhys has informed me that, due to your hard work and effort in the early stages of construction, the walls were completed far earlier than expected." Bill looked satisfied and preened with looks from his fellow masons.

"They've set up a picket line and surrounded the castle." Yand cast a stony gaze around the group. "I expect they will call for reinforcements, a proper army, to counteract any troops the King will send to defend it. They will fail. We will keep hold of this castle and hold it to the last man for, ladies and gentlemen, your very life depends on it."

Uneasy glances. Hands clutched at loved ones, and little children burrowed into the dresses of their mothers. Sam didn't relish the thought of death, and the death of innocents was even worse. These children had done nothing wrong, they were only born to the parents that brought them here.

He had to wonder if it was really as bad as everyone said it was.

Captain Yand cocked his head to the side. "In that light, you have all now been conscripted into the King's service. You will fight under me." Yand's eyes locked on Sam's. "Or you will die."

14

KNIGHT SHIFT

Sam bore the look and gave some in return. Now he was in the fire, there was no escaping it.

"We will start by dividing you up into squads. Each squad will be led by a guardsman with the proper knowledge of fighting and defense, and all of them will report directly to me."

While Yand was talking, Sam wondered where Duke Horn-blood was. He should be out here, not his stand in by proxy. Was he holed up out of fear or cowardice?

Or was there something else going on? He couldn't say one way or the other.

Glancing down at Kerien, and his ashen face, he realized he might have been too hard on the young man. Saying words was one thing, but having to live them out was quite another.

He put a hand on his shoulder. Kerien glanced over, then dropped his head. Sam let his hand slip away, hoping for the best.

"Overseer, if you please?" Yand stepped aside. The Overseer took his place. He cleared his throat and unrolled a scrap of parchment.

"Here are the assignments. First squad to be led by Guardsman Hale. Come up as I call your name." Names echoed along the silent courtyard, bouncing off the walls and tolling like bells.

A song for the dead. Despite the thick walls and the strong defensive position, Sam had mixed feelings about their future.

Would those names be read as heroes who had perished? Or would they be the names of the survivors who fought and saved themselves?

He looked down. His soup had grown cold, and he pushed it around. The others had abandoned theirs as well.

His appetite was gone. The seriousness of the situation struck him then. There was no getting out of it now, nowhere to run.

Kerien was called out of the group of carpenters, and in a daze, stepped forward to join the growing group of men.

The second squad took Ned, and Archie too. His wife clutched at him, trying to hold him back, but he gave her a forlorn look and broke free to join his new squad, standing beside Ned.

There were about fifteen in each group so far, and the Overseer began the next one.

"Sam Freeman." The first name, assigned to Guardsman Heath.

He walked through the crowd, which parted for him. A long string of masons joined him, and the blacksmith's apprentice, Brent. Then it was over, and fourteen men surrounded him.

"Bill, master mason." He strode forward, seemingly careless of his fate, but a slight hiccup in his step betrayed him. Sam watched Bill stand in his group, congratulating masons as they joined him with handshakes and hearty welcome.

And then the Overseer called Trent.

Sam felt his heart drop. The boy walked forward nervously. *This can't be happening like this.*

Bill gave Trent a cool stare, then sent a smirk towards Sam. Of all the men who had to be with Trent...

Sam shook his head. They finished the rest, a fifth squad that took the remaining men, including Dale the blacksmith.

"You'll get to know your squad leaders better."

"First squad will take the first watch," Yand said, taking over from the Overseer. "Watches will be explained to you, and training will be required for everyone. We're at war now. I suggest you act like it."

The Overseer rolled up his parchment, turned, and walked into the keep with Captain Yand to leave them all in the deepening twilight.

Heath welcomed them, but Sam was too distracted to pay much attention. He kept thinking of those days filled with blood and death, how he could never seem to escape them, no matter how hard he tried.

"Sam, are you paying attention?"

"Hmm? Yes, I am," Sam said, registering the question. A few of the masons sniggered.

"None of that now." They were huddled around in a tight circle, and the smell of unwashed bodies and sweat was strong. The masons reeked of mortar and lime. It was in their clothes and on their shoes, if they were lucky enough to have them. Heath continued. He was a competent guard, and a semi-confident man.

Sam felt bad for him, being thrust into this position. No doubt he would prefer to live life as a simple man. He struck Sam that way.

"As I was saying." A quick glance at Sam. "We'll be taking up the next watch. It will be in the middle of the night, so you need to be ready. They'll send a runner around to wake everybody after the night moon has passed."

"We don't get sleep?" Someone called out. Sam didn't know his name, he was new to the castle and worked in the quarry most of the time. Almost all those masons were unknown to him, slaving away all day breaking rock to be carted back to the castle.

"You'll get sleep tomorrow. That is, unless you'd rather have your throat slit in the night?" The comment stopped any comments that might have been coming. "The Belmarch will do it too, given the chance."

"How long is the watch?" Another mason. Sam didn't know his name either.

"A few hours."

"Will we have weapons?" Sam asked.

Heath paled a little, then shifted his weight from foot to foot. "About that... You'll have to call for help if you see anything out of place. I'll be there on the walls too, so if you need anything you can ask me."

"Weapons would be nice, in the event of an attack." Sam kept up the pressure, not sure if it was a good idea. A weapon in his hand might be worthwhile. Another in the hands of those surrounding him... might be a different story.

But it was too late. The words were spoken, the question asked. It wasn't possible to take it back, even if he wanted to.

"No weapons, not until training is complete."

"Training? I thought we were done with that." This one he did know, a weaselly mason by the name of Brough. They were murmuring and whispering to each other now.

Heath brought up his hands. "None of that, everyone will have their say in due time. Captain Yand will be leading the exercises, and we'll be teaching you everything you need to know."

"It's a little late for that." The voice was angry and belonged to a man with an angry face. "If we wanted to be soldiers, we would have signed up for that."

It was uncomfortable to have so much in common with the masons, but Sam felt it. He agreed, but kept his mouth shut. Some of the others, however, didn't.

Looking a bit taken aback, Heath screwed up his face and stood up. "Quiet." He spoke with more confidence and found his footing. "Duke Hornblood has declared martial law. That's why you're under me now, and as squad leader, I can mete out punishment as I see fit." He glared at them. "And punishment will be severe for those who disobey and incite others to disobey. The lash will be waiting for those who don't listen to me, or the gallows. Take your pick, you grubs."

Dead silence.

"Dismissed." Heath turned on a heel and marched off to the guardhouse.

Grumbles and complaints were aired, but not until he was out of earshot, then the group dispersed.

Sam was left to wonder how things were going to change, and if they were going to last long enough for him to taste that lash.

He yawned and shivered. Sam clutched at the cloak surrounding him, surprised at how chilly the brisk night air had become.

A fire burned in the Square. Too far for bow shot, the Belmarch warriors had set up camp right in the middle of the burned shacks and shanties he had called home for months.

He thought about the good things that had happened there. The meals, the dances, the celebrations as the wall was finished. Good food, good company.

And the losses as well. Men he had known for too long, and some too short. Gone, taken away from this world to the next.

He wondered if he was going to be next.

Blinking, he tried to stay awake. The watch had come too soon, the messenger shaking him too quick. He had been groggy, and traces of it still lingered.

Leaning against the side of the wall, he took a closer look down the edge.

It was a long way down, and for a moment he had a quick moment of vertigo. Light from the moon shone down on the cleared land just beneath him.

A ditch was supposed to be dug there, an additional defense designed to make it harder to get a siege tower close to the wall, but, like so many other things, there wasn't enough manpower to do it and it had been put off.

Everything was quiet, and an owl hooted in the distance.

The stone was hard, but it was more comfortable than standing. Sam's eyelids felt heavy, then shut.

He snapped them open, then rubbed them to get out the sleep. A step back took him out of danger. There would already be one man at the whipping post tomorrow, no sense in adding his own flesh.

Instead, he looked up and down the wall. These men weren't cut out to be guards and defenders, and were having trouble staying awake. However, the recent news of the previous watch had put some fear into them and they seemed to be doing well.

A few more hours and it would all be over.

Sam walked some, watching the forms move and turn around the campfire far away.

He couldn't help but analyze them, no matter how hard he tried.

Their tents were up well, but the spacing was off and they could have been more in line. They were haphazard, suggesting that the commander of this group wasn't used to encampments.

Rookie, perhaps. Or more likely, he cared little about discipline and sharp lines and more about death and destruction.

Of that, he had his doubts. He thought he had seen men out gathering wood, but that was before the sun went down and it had been hard to see.

Now, however, they had men away and posted as sentries. *They watch us and we watch them*. He couldn't make out their eyes this far away, but he knew it was true.

If he was in charge of them, he would have posted sentries in the forest too, but he had looked hard and had seen no sign of them. That meant they were either not there or so disciplined they refused to be seen.

Time would tell, and Sam hoped it was the former. They might have a fighting chance were it the case.

He scratched at his beard. He had grown used to shaving in the morning, but with the excitement he hadn't found the time. It was growing in thick and itchy, a time he disliked the most. A few more days and it would be fine, or a quick shave if he could sneak it in.

Someone shifted to his right, and another coughed farther down the wall. He had been assigned a small portion, just enough to walk and keep moving, but not enough to feel comfortable.

Sam did a few laps, trying to bring some feeling back into his legs. His shoes were already worn, and the sole was in danger of holes. It wasn't pleasant on the cold, hard stone.

Something caught his eye in the forest. Sam blinked away his tiredness, then focused on the spot.

A puff of breeze shook the trees, but other than that, all he could hear were his compatriots on the wall. One shuffled his feet, another coughed.

There was something out there, he was sure of it. All his exhaustion fled at once, and he was alert as his heart kicked into action.

Out of the dark woods, as quiet as a fox on the prowl, men slipped out and started the long trek across open territory to the wall.

They were carrying ladders.

"Attack! To the wall." Sam's voice rang in the courtyard, and the enemy burst into a sprint.

15

GRASS ON THE PLAIN

The alarm bell rang in the night, clear and loud. The attackers were at the wall already, and there was no one with a weapon in sight.

The ladders dug into the ground, then started a long ascent up. First one, then another.

Sam looked around, desperate for something to keep them at bay. Swords and blades glinted in the hands of the men below, and they looked ready to use them.

Guardsman Heath was running, buckling his belt, to get to the stairs. He was shouting, telling them to repel the invaders.

If it wasn't so serious, Sam would have laughed. Repel them with what? A chunk of wood?

The thought struck him. Bit by bit, the ladders came closer, pushed by the men below. There were dozens all the camp as far as he knew.

And there were less than ten here, converging on the same spot. "Check the other sides, they might be coming from different directions."

Sam sprinted to the stairs. Heath was at the top, panting. "They're using ladders. We need to push them off, do you have anything that can do that?"

"Spears, down below. They're coming with them."

"That's not enough, and they won't get here in time. What else do you have?"

Heath ran to the edge, then swallowed hard. "There are so many."

Sam took him in his arms and spun him around. "Think. Do you have anything long?"

"No...I don't know."

He let him go and growled. "You two, come with me."

"Go," Heath said, dazed. Sam ran down the stairs, careful not to trip, and ran for the wood. It was farther than he would like, but they were there before the guards started streaming out of the keep.

"Take these." Sam pulled out long, square pieces of wood, almost like poles. He handed them to the two masons who followed, and took one for himself. "Up the wall."

They ran back. Sam's heart was thumping, and the extra weight wasn't helping anything. The night was cool and smelled fresh, but he knew if they didn't hurry, it would be filled with blood.

They beat the guards, who were trying to rush in behind them. Sam took the steps two at a time.

When he reached the top, an attacker was over the wall. Heath was fighting with him, sword drawn and flashing.

It wasn't a fair fight, and before Sam could do anything about it, the wicked-looking blade took Heath across the shoulder.

Desperate, Sam swung the pole as Heath dropped, giving him enough room to go over his head.

The man opened his mouth in surprise, but didn't duck in time. A shudder went down the pole and up Sam's arms to his shoulders. He heard a crunch, then the man flew over the side of the wall to his right.

A clatter next to him distracted him from another attacker as he popped his head over the wall.

"Push it off," Sam bellowed. A guard rushed by him as he stopped to shove his pole against the ladder rung. Grunting and straining, Sam dug into the stones of the wall and pushed with all his might.

It was heavy. Someone must have been on it. Hands took the pole, joining him, and added strength.

The ladder creaked and moved backward, inch by inch. It shook and shivered, and a head appeared.

It reached the tipping point and swung back. The man on it shrieked as it fell backward with a crash.

Gasping for breath, Sam leaned on the pole. "Push them off the wall."

Guards rushed past him, attacking the two men who managed to get up the other ladder. More clatters as another found a perch.

There was shouting, a clash of sword, and screams. A guardsman stabbed a ladder climber, who fell down onto the man behind him.

Sam saw his opening and rushed in, pushing the ladder away.

Shouts from the other side of the wall. There was another group trying the same thing on the west side.

They had all three poles in use, pushing. The guards sheathed sword, rolling the bodies of the attackers away, and joined them in pushing another away.

Another three ladder attacks, and they pushed them all away.

"Take two to the other side." The courtyard was ablaze with activity now. Sam pushed two members of his squad toward the other side of the wall. When he was sure they were going, he handed his pole off to another group and knelt down beside Heath.

He was still alive and coughed as Sam rolled him over.

"Stay with me now." Sam grasped his hand. It was warm and slippery. Blood trickled from the corner of Heath's mouth.

He reeked of it, and fear. "Did we stop them?" His voice was weak and halting. Sam looked down.

There was nothing he could do.

"We stopped them. Thanks to you. You're a brave man, Heath." The only one with a weapon, but brave enough to face a hardened soldier on his own.

"I'm glad." Life was draining from his eyes. Sam held on tight as Heath clung to him. "I don't want to die."

"I know." Sam fought back tears as the last of his life left, and his body gave up its spirit.

The hand went limp, and Sam let it drop from his own. Such a young man, less than thirty summers old. Taken away in the blink of an eye.

Sam closed his unseeing eyes and murmured a prayer over him. The rest of the world came back in focus for him.

Yelling, screaming, cursing, the men fought to keep the ladders off the wall. Arrows were flying up now, and some found their mark.

However, the guards were sending them back in return as well. Even with only one pole, they were able to keep them back, and some threw whatever they could find. Rock, chunks of the wall, they tossed them at the attackers where they could.

Sam knew it would be over soon. They'd had their chance, and now it was gone. If only they could burn their ladders, that would stop them.

For a time.

He had no doubt there would be more attempts, more ladders. They would need more than sticks to defend the castle.

Captain Yand was surveying the fight, blood dripping off his sword.

"Archers to the west wall," he said.

Sam felt his age now. A younger man would have kept up, but he was past his prime.

"They'll be back," he said, leaning up against the wall. "How long do you think we can keep this up without weapons?"

Yand glanced at him, his eyes flashing in the moonlight. "Empty words from a man who refuses to fight."

"And yet they weigh your heart."

"I am in charge of the defenses of this fortress, carpenter, not you." He wiped the blood off his sword on his pants. He must have been the one to kill the attacker. "Will you advise the Duke on matters of state next?"

The momentary image of him whispering in the young Duke's ear brought him some levity, but didn't change the situation they were in.

"It's only a matter of time before they have more troops and more siege weapons. How can you hope to hold out when that happens?"

Yand gave him a cold look, then returned his gaze to the battlefield below. The archers were having an effect now. With a perfect vantage point from the wall, they landed arrow after arrow among the attackers.

Some lay still on the ground, unmoving. Far more than Heath.

This attack had cost them, and would cost them more.

Faced with the continued repulsion of their ladders, the Belmarch were starting to retreat.

"They run now. They will run tomorrow." Captain Yand sheathed his sword and stood against the wall, leaning out over the edge. The ladders were left in the field, splayed out like sticks in a forest.

Yand turned and swept his cloak over his shoulder. He walked past Sam, then stopped. Over his shoulder he said, "You wish for weapons. You may have your wish granted yet."

A chill ran down Sam's back. Memories flushed to the surface of his mind. Unpleasant, horrible memories. Someone groaned from down below, another victim in a senseless war.

Yand continued, walking briskly to the gatehouse. He was probably going to the other side, where the yells and clashes were still continuing. They were struggling to push back the ladders.

There were more over there, and Sam got to his feet and ran down the stairs. A flush crept up his cheeks, even despite the chilliness of the night.

His blood was up and warm. He didn't know why, what had set it off, but it was there. Being called a coward, he could deal with.

Something didn't sit right with him.

Step after step he ran, passed the waiting women and a few children that had been woken by the noise.

They called to him, asked for news, but he ignored it and took the steps up, joining them just in time to add his weight to a pole.

Together, they pushed it off. It clattered on the rocks below with an accompanied scream. Bows twanged and arrows flew.

Another ladder. Another repulsion. A few more and they had had enough. The ladders stopped being lifted, and the Belmarch fled.

Yand had arrived, and was directing the mop up. Sam caught his breath, resting on the edge of the wall.

A few more arrows found their mark, but they were only wounding shots. They ran till they were out of range, then limped the rest of the way, carrying their wounded and leaving their dead.

Regrouping, the Belmarch huddled together in a mass and turned back to their encampment. The defenders on the wall let out a cheer. Sam knew it would be short-lived and let them. They were clapping hands, congratulating themselves on a job well done.

Few wounded on this side of the wall. They must have been slower, for the slope was steeper on this side. Or they had been seen earlier.

Either way, the end of the battle had come and gone.

"Settle down," Yand said, his booming voice echoing. "They may be licking their wounds tonight, but we lost good men. Keep your silence for them."

Smiles faded away, the joy of the evening gone. Hats were removed and held in hands, and everyone looked back to the stairs.

They were carrying his body down, two men at the feet and one at the head. Heath had gone stiff already.

Sam looked back to the enemy, too overcome to try and remain calm. There was a figure in the distance, at the tree line. He was large and imposing, standing off to the side.

He watched them from afar. Sam could feel his gaze, could smell the sweat and hate flowing from him.

He set his chin on the cool rock. It dug into his skin, but he didn't care. It was a feeling, it was real.

It took him away from thoughts he had wished were left far behind, from a past he had tried to escape.

"Everyone not on watch, back to sleep. Take care of what you need to tonight and be prepared for tomorrow." Yand turned to the guardsman beside him. "Squad leaders, take charge."

He strode off, back to the keep. Sam had no doubt he would sleep well tonight, not like many in this castle.

"Third squad, we're taking over," Dawain said. He was in charge of them.

"What do we do? Heath's gone now," a mason said. Sam shook his head. Come and gone, a flash of bright light and extinguished a second later.

It brought his own fire inside, fueling it.

"Heath's squad, you clean up, collect the arrows, then get some sleep. I'll be in charge until the morning."

They scattered, collecting up the groups of arrows that had been brought out by the guards during the attack. Bows were unstrung and were carried back with the rest of the weapons and guardsman to the keep. Sam carried a few bundles with him to store in the armory outside when Trent ran up to him. "What happened?" His eyes were wide and wild. "They kept us inside, wouldn't tell us what was happening."

Foolish. "They attacked, as you can see." Sam walked by, but Trent turned and kept up.

Heath was in the courtyard now, laid to rest, and had been covered by a blanket. "We stopped them. For now."

"How did they do it? Was it difficult to keep them away?"

"Trent, I'm tired. No more questions, please. We'll talk about it in the morning." Trent fell back beside him, still but trailing a few feet. "

His tone had been too sharp. He should apologize.

But all he wanted to do was sleep now, and if a few harsh words had helped that, it was worth it.

"I'll see you in the morning. I can answer your questions, then."

"Goodnight." Trent walked off, back to the keep. Most of the women had gone back in, corralling their children with them. The stillness of the night was coming back as they did.

Sam returned the arrows and looked up into the night sky. Stars twinkled, wisps of clouds obscuring them as they moved across the world.

He would have no peace here.

16

FOLLY OR COWARDICE

Hands lifted the rough locking bar, pulling it out of the braces. Quietly, they moved it and set it down. A few dabs of oil on the hinges made the door as silent as it could be, but it still creaked.

The sound seemed deafening to the workers, and they held their breath. Watching, waiting, they kept going when it was clear there were none who heard it.

The portcullis was trickier. Three men worked to raise it, cloths and linens wrapped around the chain that pulled it up, but there was no way to hide it. The sound rang clear in the deep still of night.

A clap on the back, and the man was out and under in a flash. Hands worked the portcullis back down, letting it shut with a soft bang. The door was next, squeaking shut and locked in less than a minute.

The man was gone, blended into the night with a dark outfit and quiet shoes.

Yand watched from the wall, wishing they had a horse to send with him. He tracked the movement along the wall, in the shadow of the night, until the man slipped into the safety of the trees.

Their hopes rested with him.

A haze settled over the castle, creeping into the walls and sticking to the stone. Tendrils of waters dripped from protrusions.

Sam breathed in the late morning air. Wet, heavy, and filled with smoke.

"Any word?"

"Nothing so far," Sam said. Ned nodded, then took a seat next to him on the wall. His joints creaked as he settled into place, legs dangling over the edge.

"It's been three days since the last attack. I thought we'd have something else by now." Sam peered over the wall through the mist. He could just make out the line of trees. They stood as giant sentinels in a line. Sounds of construction drifted across the expanse from time to time.

"The Duke's been out to see the womenfolk," Ned said.

"Oh?" Sam shifted.

"Wants to reassure them something is going to be done. That they'll have a battalion of fighters coming any day now."

"Good news then."

"Well..." Ned turned to the makeshift shacks they had constructed. Families were huddled beneath them, waiting.

For what, no one knew.

"Captain Yand is a fierce fighter. He'll have a plan." Sam checked his bow again, still wondering how they had managed it. Another weapon in his hands.

Could he use it? Other than at practice?

Bales of hay were one thing, a human target quite another.

"How is Trent doing?"

Ned shifted and was silent for far too long. Sam cursed silently. "He's holding up."

"They beat him, don't they?"

"They call it training. Bill's convinced him of that."

Flashes of anger drifted across his vision. The fog lifted for a second, blown by a stray bit of wind, then settled back before he could get a better look at their encampment. "I want to tear him limb from limb sometimes."

"I know what you mean."

"I thought not having the pressure of construction would help, that he would ease off of us." He tightened his grip on the bow. "I was wrong."

"The Overseer protects him still." Ned shrugged. "Even with his thefts of extra rations."

"A punishable offense," Sam quoted. "Who is there to judge the law in this place?" he looked into the sky. Fog obscured the clouds.

"Not us, I'm afraid. It was never us to begin with." After a pause, Ned continued. "I'm too old for this, Sam." There was a weariness in his voice that shocked him. Sam looked to him.

"No one has asked for this."

"You're right about that. No one has. Even though I knew it might happen, I still came. A long life lived, I'm now at the end of it."

"You aren't giving up, are you?"

"Not quite yet."

"The Ned I know wouldn't give up as easy as that. There's still plenty of forest. Wood to work, things to build."

"I've spent my life building to make amends for the things I've destroyed. I thought it would make the world right again." He stood up, brushed off his pants. "It turns out all of life is vanity."

Like a knife in his heart, Sam felt the words bore into him. What kind of damaged had he done? Lives lost, lives ended.

"Is there any cause for hope?" Sam whispered the words, more to himself than anyone else.

"We all have things we're running from." Ned put a hand on his shoulder, gazed into his eyes with sad, drooping eyes, and turned. He creaked down the steps, leaving Sam alone at his watch and alone in his heart.

The sound of hammers striking something large brought him to the wall. The air was clear, and visibility was unlimited to the enemy encampment.

The trees were beginning to turn, gold and brown creeping in on the oaks. It was only a matter of time until autumn would come at last.

"What are they doing?" A man sidled next to him, leaning on his bow.

"Don't do that," Sam replied after a quick glance.

"Do what?"

"You'll break the bow, leaning on it like that." The man, startled, let go and stood up. Philip, if Sam recalled right.

"Sorry." Sam was probably harsher than he had right to be, but the long nights and lack of sleep was starting to get to him. The training, too, wasn't as easy as it might have been once. "So, do you know what it is?"

"A catapult." The machine was obvious, even from this far away. The spoon shaped arm, the bracing that led to wheels. They were planning on using it to take down the wall, if he had a guess.

And off to the side, somewhere hidden in the bushes or behind the trees, they had a battering ram. Of that, he was sure.

Crude lines and mismatched joints aside, the catapult looked like it would only take a few more days to be operational. After that, it was only a matter of time before they were using it to batter the walls and bring them down.

Philip sucked in a breath, then let out a low whistle. Absent-mindedly, he almost leaned on the bow again, but then caught himself after a sharp look at Sam. "What are they going to do with it?"

"Throw rocks at us, more than likely. They'll be too far from our bows for us to do anything about it." Sam surveyed the courtyard again. All the building materials had been cleared to the side to make room for training.

Stacks of stone ran up against the west wall. Some were cut, others fresh from the quarry. Work had halted on the keep until the siege was over.

Crates, foodstuffs, and other supplies were around the smith, including the rest of his fuel. Their stacks of firewood were dwindling despite the rationing. It was taking a lot of it to cook the food.

That made him glance nervously at their supply of lumber. Good, hard lumber that had been seasoned more than a year already. He had seen the eyes looking at it, devouring it, thinking about burning it next.

A foul taste rose in his mouth, the more he thought about it, the sicker he was going to get.

He wanted them to keep their hands off it, to leave their hard work alone. No one was going to burn the stones of the masons for all the work they put into shaping it and cutting it. Those rocks would be like that for the next hundred years or more.

"Sounds bad," Philip said, recapturing his attention. Sam turned back to the enemy. They were pounding something in place at the back. Something with the arm, perhaps? He didn't know.

It had been too quiet this last week. No attacks, no new arrivals, nothing. They just sat there, waiting for them and pillaging the crops they had planted.

His stomach grumbled at the thought. He would give anything for a fresh chunk of venison right now.

Or a fresh vegetable.

The thought of it, fresh and cool. A cucumber, crunchy with juice dripping down his chin. He pushed the thought away. It would do no good.

"We aren't in the best of circumstances right now."

"Give it time, your Lordship. The messenger needs to get to Whitehall." The Overseer sat in front of the desk while the young Duke stood over him.

"You said it would take a week at most to get there. Surely the King would have sent word by the fastest means possible." His hair was disheveled, his shirt ruffled.

"We had no birds to send with him. We must wait for the slow word," the Overseer said, trying his best to be cool and calm, to infuse his voice with the same. A smile was plastered to his face, stuck there with pure will.

"I would advise patience as well, sire." Yand was standing with his hands behind his back, watching the Overseer carefully. His steely eyes held something behind them.

"I expect the King to send a battalion. How long would it take to get here?"

The Overseer and Captain Yand looked at each other. The Overseer clamped his mouth shut.

Yand held up his chin. "With the...turmoil in the Kingdom at present, aid might be...underwhelming."

The Duke spun on his heel. "What have you been hiding?" He leveled a glare at the fighter, one that belied his station but not his age.

"Hiding? Nothing, sire. News in the Kingdom travels fast, I thought you knew about the raiders to the east?"

"I knew about them."

"And that they have diverted the majority of the King's forces?" Silence. "That the men at arms were raised to march on them and restore peace, but they did not find easy ways?"

The Overseer cleared his throat. "I have heard the same. The brigands fight well, and hide in the hills, harnessing our forces. Rumors are that the King will ride on them himself with his own forces."

The Duke stopped, then sat in his chair. "And there will be enough left for us? To defend against a far greater threat?"

"This threat is an incursion at present, your lordship." A cloud descended on the Duke's face at those words.

"Incursion? A Duke, trapped in his own castle with no way to leave, is merely an incursion?"

"They have no reinforcements as of yet," Yand said. The Overseer breathed a quick breath of relief as the Duke turned on him.

"They kill my men and keep me locked away, is that not enough for the King to send aid?"

"I hope it is," the Overseer said, then added quickly, as the glower was lowered to him, "Belmarch is preoccupied as a whole. Some might see this as a spearhead designed to land more forces, others might see it as an opportune time to raid and pillage. We have walls to protect us, and men to man them. It is possible the raiders will leave, given enough time."

"And when would that be? When they have eaten every-thing in our fields?" Red was creeping up the Duke's neck. "When they have stripped our forests bare, destroyed our quarry? They aim to kill us and take this fortress as their own. They will march an army across and ravage our land."

The other two said nothing. Yand stared straight ahead, the Overseer was locked in his most ingratiating look.

"I can tell you don't agree." The Duke sat back, the anger falling away from him. "Speak your mind."

"We may be on our own," Yand said. "And there may be no help to be had. We should plan accordingly."

"And you, Overseer Rhys?"

"I prefer to be behind well-defended and strong walls. Men who are cautious are bound to lead long lives."

"So this is it, then?" The Duke looked from one to the other. "I must choose between folly and cowardice?"

17

CRAFTING

Sweat poured down his face, stinging his eyes and dripping off his eyebrows in distracting drops. Sam dove left, narrowly avoiding a blow, and countered with a weak attack to the left hip.

Trent saw it and shifted mid swing to twist out of the way. *Better than last time*. He followed up with a strike to the ribcage.

That blow landed and was less held back than the one before.

Groaning, Trent took another step back, kicking up dust and rock as he did. The training ground was emptier than it had been, but still reeked of sweat from the men.

Sam spat away the salty sweat. "You're learning."

"Not fast enough." Trent held his side. Sam chuckled and twisted his sword around. "Another round?"

"Not tonight." He wasn't used to this, and his muscles were telling him. The aches were less than the first few nights, but they weren't pleasant.

Trent nodded and offered a hand to take the practice sword. Sam handed it over and let him take it to the Keep.

"The lad is doing well. I wondered who was teaching him." Bill stepped out from the shadows of the lean-to far back behind the wall.

Sam turned, cursing himself for not noticing earlier. "You refuse to teach him anything, don't you?"

"We teach him enough." Bill leaned up against the wooden pole. Sam's hand instinctively clutched at his side.

At a sword not there.

He breathed, trying to calm his palpitating heart. What good would getting angry do?

Still, he had seen the bruises when Trent hadn't noticed and was taking off his shirt. Well-hidden underneath his clothes.

Not ones Sam had given him in their nightly sessions.

"There are lessons to be given," Sam said, stalking to the right. His eyes slipped over the area, looking for something to defend himself if the need arose.

"Oh, that there are." Bill grinned wickedly. "Lessons to never be forgotten indeed."

"Where are your friends now, Bill? Hiding, waiting to ambush me when the time is right?" Sam couldn't see any of them, if they were in the shadows, they were well hidden.

"Just me. Wanted to hear if the rumors were true. Seems kind of unusual that a carpenter would know how to teach a young boy swordsmanship, don't you think?"

Sam shrugged, continuing to circle. "I'm good with a blade. Must come naturally."

"I think you're hiding something."

"Aren't you?"

"Don't change the subject."

"How is it that Bill, a nobody, manages to become head stonemason building the Hornbloods a castle?" Bill's grin faded a little. "Oh yes, we can talk about rumors if you'd like. About trying to get out of places that are designed for bad people who do bad things." Sam stopped and turned his head. "Oh, how are the dungeons coming along, anyway?"

Crickets chirped in the grass. The night was dark, devoid of moonlight, but the stars shimmered in the black blanket of the sky. It was getting late, he needed to go back to his own bed.

"I suggest you stay away from me, if you know what's good for you, and focus on the problem at hand." Sam jerked a thumb behind him. "A very nasty problem that can slide a blade between your ribs before you get a chance to use that dagger hidden in your boot."

Bill pulled his left leg back. *So that was it.* "I'll remember everything you did to me."

"If that was a problem, I hope you would have a better memory. Goodnight Bill." Sam turned and walked away, going at a reasonable, uncaring pace, despite the man wielding more than a grudge behind him.

He didn't know where Bill went, probably back to his own special hut that he had his masons build, despite Sam's objections.

He, however, didn't care. He might have made things worse between them, that was true, but there were more important things to worry about than a petty feud between two men.

As he slipped through the doors, joining the rest of the sleeping forms in the great hall, he had a momentary pang of regret. How was badgering Bill supposed to make him an ally?

He undressed and slipped into the small covering they called a bed. A few men were snoring, but most were just asleep. Trent was bundled up in the corner, at least Sam thought he was.

The families had their own places now. Rough, unglamorous places to gather, but enough to keep them out of the rain and wind sheltered by the wall on one side.

Now, the great hall was filled with the bachelors, all except Bill, of course, who had his own special place of rock and stone.

That man was infuriating, and more dangerous than everyone else thought him to be.

The thought of how to handle him stayed with him, keeping him up. He stayed awake for a long time.

Sam picked over the wood, turning each piece in his hand. he looked down one edge, checking for twists and cracks. He needed a good, straight piece for this.

Finally, he found one. A thick piece of ash that smelled seasoned and was coated in a thin layer of dust. He knocked it off, then scraped a corner off to reveal the grain.

Straight, and no knots or defects he could see. It would do.

A steady drizzle of rain was coming down outside. Small holes in the ceiling let in drips, and the workshop had been arranged to account for these. Piles of wood were shifted, and buckets were placed in the worst spots. The others dripped into the dirt and made mud.

It had been a while since he had done any work here, being on a rotating shift of watching and training. He didn't know how long he could pretend anymore, and it was weighing on him.

He took the wood and split off the chunk he needed. Long, straight, about two inches thick by two inches wide. Six feet long, at least, and more than enough to do what he wanted it to do.

He prepared the cut piece, shaving off the sides and marking his width. He did the same to the other side. The plane rasped along the edge, a ribbon of broken wood flying from the end of it.

It fell with a whisper, letting out the smell of the wood like a perfume that filled the leaking workshop. The others were gone, leaving him to work alone.

Sam couldn't recall the last time he had worked alone, but he enjoyed it.

The shavings fell, then he turned it on its corner. A few more planes turned it into a flat.

Continuing with the other sides, he carved it into an octagon. He checked it after he was done. It was still straight and smooth. Ready for the lathe.

He set it up, chucking it between the jaws and wrapping around the leather cord that served as the power source.

A few pumps on the pedal got it spinning, and he lightly touched the gouge to the edge, running it along down the length.

Wood peeled off in chunks, sputtering and spraying. When they came out as whole shavings, he moved down the pole.

It took a few moves of the lathe, but eventually that octagon turned into a smooth cylinder.

A few rubs with the fine sand and it was polished, ready for the final step. It was not his act that would finish this piece, but someone else.

Sam laid it across the workbench, then stepped back. A storm raged in his mind as the gentle rain showered outside.

He was confused. He didn't know what to do or how to do it. And, worst of all, he was trapped here.

Trapped, like always. And no matter what he seemed to do, it always seemed to make things worse.

He breathed in the fresh scent of the air, then let it out. Closing his eyes, he repeated a training he had learned long ago.

Release. Breathe. Hold. Exhale.

Over and over again, until the storm settled some. *Concentrate on the breath, let everything else go.*

He thought making something would calm him, but here he was, nearly at dinnertime, and he was just as agitated.

The bell rang, breaking him out of his concentration. He took up his cloak and threw it over his shoulders, pulling the hood up to keep out the rain.

Smoke trailed from the chimney of the keep. The kitchens were working today, of that he could have no doubt.

Which meant warm food. His heart lightened a little. The past few days they were served the remains of what was left uncooked, hard breads locked away into barrels that would break your teeth and tasted about the same, and the rest of the cheeses before they were too moldy.

They had to scrape the rest off. There would be no more milk or cheese, not with the animals left outside the walls.

Sam was sure they were long gone, slaughtered to fill the bellies of the attackers.

"What's good?" He slipped in behind Ned at the back of the line.

"Mush, from what they're saying up ahead." He didn't sound lighthearted, but Sam couldn't blame him for that. Who could, in conditions like these?

"Oh, I thought it would be something else. Something mo re…"

"Cooked?" Kerien asked. Sam nodded. "We might get some bread, if the rumors are true. Martha baked some with flour ground from a mill that the masons cut for her."

"So there is a bright spot." He could remember Martha's bread. Soft, warm, fluffy on the inside and a delightful crunch on the outside, slathered with butter that melted into golden heaven.

Reality was far more different. It was gruel, ground up oats in water cooked until they were mush, and a small roll to go with it.

He pressed a thumb into his. Sam was glad it went in, not as hard as the biscuits had been, but not as soft as he remembered it.

They were good, but would have paired better with butter, or a haunch of pig.

Sam ate with the other carpenters, listening to their tales of woe and pain as he did.

"I can't seem to sleep, with all the waking up in the middle of the night to go to watch." Kerien had bags under his eyes, dark black, and they gazed with a semi-blank look.

"Sleep? My legs are so sore I can't even think about it," Trent said, rubbing them. "There's too much training and lugging stone around."

"What do you have to do that for?" Ned asked.

"Prepare for attacks. Although they keep moving the locations."

"Locations?" Something tickled the back of Sam's thought.

"Last night it was the west wall, but today they said it was the south wall."

"What are you talking about, Trent?" Kerien stared at him.

The boy looked around at them, eyes wide. "The rocks, don't you have to move them during your watch? Well, at night I mean."

"I haven't had to move rocks," Kerien said, then returned to his meal to scoop the last little bit out of his bowl.

"Neither have we," Archie said.

"They have you move piles of rocks in the night?" Sam asked.

"Yes."

"There is no reason to do that. Bill is playing with you again." Ned's expression hardened, but Kerien smiled.

"You haven't been falling for that, have you?" His eyes twinkled malevolently.

"They said..."

"Guardsman Sal didn't tell you that, did he? It was Bill, wasn't it?" Trent looked down and kicked the ground.

Somehow, this made everything Bill had done worse. Toying with a young boy, making him do useless tasks.

Sam was going to have a word with Bill about it, and he would have that word soon.

Had he known this before, the night might have turned out differently last night.

The bell rang, a voice shouting out over the noise.

Everyone went silent and listened to it. They put down their meals and rushed to their assigned areas.

By now, everyone knew where to go, unlike before. It had been chaos, with confused men running around like chickens chased by a fox.

They fell into lines, waiting as the guardsmen rushed out of the barracks, already dressed and ready for the attack.

Yand strode across the courtyard, bellowing orders. His eyes met Sam's, and then they slipped away.

"We've got another fight to take to the enemy, men. Don't let me down now."

18

THE MESSEGE

Enemy torches blazed on the horizon, arrayed in a group around the creaking and trundling catapult. They were geared up and ready to fight, with war paint and gleaming armor.

The entire castle seemed to be out on the walls, including women and children near the back. Captain Yand whispered something to the head guard, and in a few moments, the guards were chasing them down, but let the men remain.

Sam took up a perch with his carpenters, an electricity in the air that he longed to reach out and touch. The feeling of it filled him with shame, but the anticipation was too much to ignore.

"They're going to attack, aren't they?" Trent asked in a hushed whisper.

"It looks that way, boy," Ned said. The rocks were still warm from the sun, and the air shimmered slightly with the haze. Fall may have come, but the weather hadn't turned cold yet.

And it was a good thing too. Sam wasn't looking forward to the freezing rain and blizzards of winter. Not like this, not as unprepared as they were.

"They're doing something there," Kerien said, pointing. All along the wall others were saying the same thing. A buzz went up of conversation, but a quick look from Yand lowered the level to a mere whisper.

They were doing something with it. It had stopped, the men pulling it dropping the ropes to the ground and hammering in stakes to the wheels. The sound drifted across the open ground, a dull, ominous sound.

Men were moving around it now, and there was some shouting. Sam shaded his eyes with a hand and squinted, trying to make out what they were doing.

He caught them loading the bucket with something, but it was small, and he couldn't see any stones around to continue the attack.

They cranked back the arm, two men heaving at the rope until it was loaded and ready.

"Here it comes." Sam ducked down, right at the top of the crenelation. Others followed suit.

An order, and the cord pulled. The great arm swung forward, faster than Sam would have expected, and slammed into the top crosspiece with a crash.

The rock flew at them, crossing yards in the blink of an eye. It sailed over their heads, then landed in the courtyard with a soft splat.

Sam crinkled his brow. "They missed those idiots!" someone shouted down the line. A great roar of laughter went up from the defenders.

"Fools, be quiet." Yand's voice cut through it all, and the cheer died away. "Do you even see what they've done? Bring it to me."

He pointed to the missile.

A guard was down in a flash. He turned when he reached it, a look of horror on his face. "It's a head."

Gasps. Someone from inside screamed, a woman in the keep. It was taken to Yand, who covered it with a cloth.

"See what they've done! These are the men we fight, not men but demons." He raised his bloody package above his head. "Prepare to repel an attack, and realize that there is no safety in surrender."

He walked down the stairs and back into the keep. Everyone was silent until he was inside, then started talking.

"They aren't doing anything." Trent was looking at the enemy.

"This was a message, not an attack." Sam looked back at the waiting troops. There was a man out front, larger than all the others. He would have no mercy, he would give no quarter. Of that, he was now certain.

"They're saying it was Jedediah, one of the fastest guardsmen." Word came down the line, passed from man to man.

"What was he doing out of the castle? Foolish," Ned said, making the sign to ward off evil.

"Not foolish, an act of desperation." Sam breathed deep of the warm autumn air. It brought fresh scents of the forest from across the river.

"What do you mean?"

"I doubt Jedediah snuck out of the castle, which means he was let out." Sam looked back to the keep. Would they be able to hold out without help? The next messenger wasn't expected for another month, at the earliest.

Thoughts raced through Sam's mind, trying to connect everything he'd seen. The conversation around him continued, and he withdrew from it.

What will the Duke do? There they were, waiting for a response. They had no response other than arrows and words, the thick walls of the castle their only real defense.

How long would that hold against a determined enemy and tons of rock chucked through a catapult? Not long, he suspected.

"They aren't attacking, so that means they don't mean us much harm, right?" Trent asked, eyes wide.

"Did you see the head they flung over the wall? They mean us plenty of harm." Kerien pushed him. Not hard, but enough to be uncalled for.

Sam gave him a stern look. Kerien shrugged. "It was a dumb question from a dumb kid."

"Not long ago I seem to remember another dumb child," Ned said, calm. His big, bushy eyebrows lowered, but his eyes were fixed on Kerien. "Fighting each other won't help anything."

"I'm not the one causing all the problems." Kerien jerked his head back toward Bill and the masons grouped around him on the wall.

They were deep in conversation, heads bent toward Bill, nearly at the center.

The ale had gone long ago, and the foul smell that normally clung to them was replaced by simple sweat and unwashed body smell. Sam didn't like the look of them, even considering what lay outside the wall.

If there was a way to just get rid of Bill, to get him out of the castle. *No, I mustn't think like that.*

"We're trapped together here. Might as well make the best of it," Ned said. He reached for his pipe, grabbed it, but then put it back in a pocket.

There was nothing to fill it with. Not anymore. The grimace on his face told Sam all he needed to know.

The bows were out and ready, handed along the squad of men on watch. They were few and far between, and not nearly enough to equip the now fledgling army of castle workers.

"We need more arms, more bows." Sam kicked himself for just thinking of it now. "We can make them with the stock we have."

"I've never made a bow before. I wouldn't know how," Archie said.

Sam looked at Ned, who shook his head. "Only once, and it didn't go well."

"We're carpenters. We work with wood. I'm sure we can make it work."

They were all silent, even as conversation surrounded them. "Do you have anything better to do?"

That got them. Construction had halted with the siege, with no way to get supplies and no reason to continue it. Survival was more important right now than a leaky roof.

"We'll give it our best," Archie said, jutting his chin out.

Sam returned his gaze back to the invaders, watching them watch the castle in return. He wondered what they were thinking, what they were planning.

They had to have a next step, and it had to result in more bloodshed and pain. Like a thorn in his flesh, the thought bothered him, dug into him deep inside.

Why couldn't they leave us alone? He wasn't a Chathem native, but he hadn't seen any aggression to the Belmarchers on his part. No thoughts of invasion, no desire to take their lands. So why is it they did?

The big man out front turned away as the sun started to set. He had given his message, his work was done. The rest of the army turned away, except for a few lone guards, and retreated back to their camp.

Something tickled Sam's mind, like a breeze on a flag.

"What are you thinking?" Ned asked.

"I don't know yet. Meet me tomorrow morning to work on the bows. I've got something I want to look at." Sam bade them goodnight, and they dispersed like the others not on watch. They were going back to their families, if they had them, or to talk amongst themselves down below. The watchers remained ready and alert in case the attackers decided to change their minds.

The Duke's room was lit, and shadows moved along the wall. He had no doubt Yand had gone there to break the bad news to him. He didn't envy the Duke right now, with an unseasoned guard and only one true fighter in the bunch he had a series of hard decisions.

One of which was surrender.

Sam picked his way along the wall, moving around the watchers scanning their areas. To those who were friendly, he greeted, to the ones who weren't he ignored.

The latter group was made mostly of masons, poisoned by the words of Bill, no doubt.

Sam shook his head, and a few moments later was at his vantage point.

It was the eastern side of the castle, the only side that abutted anything but the forest. The Golden River flowed right below, built on the rocks that made up the bank.

It was quiet and calm. The river trickled and moved underneath that top exterior. The wall was over forty feet above it on this side, plenty of space to prevent boats from attacking and scaling the wall.

He looked down. The water wasn't directly below him, that was reserved for the rocky bank. Anything that dropped down there from this height would be crushed and shattered upon them.

But what if they could get a little farther out...

He tried to judge the distance, moving along the wall to find the shortest length of bank. It was about halfway down. The one guard assigned to this side of the castle watched him with a curious look.

A few feet, ten at most. That was all that separated them from the river.

Sam sat, dangling his legs over the side of the wall, and thought. A thin wind blew over him, ruffling his hair and bringing with it the smell of the river and forest. Leaves were starting to change on the other side, hints of brown among the green.

They were in a bad position. With no help on the way, it would only be a matter of time before the Belmarchers would reinforce their numbers. They would get the upper hand eventually, whittle away the defenders one by one if they needed to.

He would never have thought he would be in this position. Sam shook his head. A foolish lack of insight in retrospect.

But now he was here.

He imagined what he would do if he was in charge. If they gave him command tomorrow. Would he sit here, waiting to be slaughtered?

Would he just accept a head thrown over the wall, a challenge that had to be responded to?

His stomach churned thinking about it. A heron swooped low over the water, chasing its reflection upriver. One eye looked beneath the calm surface.

A second later the beak flashed, struck, and water splashed. It never broke flight, but a wriggling, struggling fish struggled in its beak.

It flew off into the gloomy twilight. Sam sat and watched until it was his turn to take the watch.

He went to the courtyard, through the ritual of guard change they had come to learn so well. A transfer of weapons, a count of the arrows. The squad leaders exchanging a few words, then they were sent to their respective section of the wall.

Sam looked over the courtyard on his way up, thinking about how they could use the slope to their advantage. The keep was finished enough to be a defensible position.

He shook his head. This wasn't his job, this wasn't his to think about. Captain Yand was in charge, and Duke Hornblood was in command. They were supposed to see the defenses, to arrange what they had to finish to stay alive.

A part of him knew that they hadn't done a good job. They had barely kept the ladder attack at bay, and a few after it, with little plan to counterattack.

He couldn't help but feel some resentment at it, that he could have done it better. A wave of fear washed over him as soon as he thought it.

He didn't know how to lead a siege, let alone defend from one.

But now he wasn't sure either one of them could either.

19

COUNCILS AND CONUNDRUMS

The Duke stared up at the emblem of his house. It was enormous, imposing.

At first he had liked it. Loved it, really. A constant reminder of where he came from and where his authority lay.

Now, however, with how things were...

"What do you mean, he came back?" A few flies buzzed around the head laying on his table. He wrinkled his nose at the smell. Decayed. Dead. At least three days, but the stench.

"That's our messenger. A guardsman, Jedediah." Captain Yand was standing at attention behind him. The Duke felt the room swirl. He could see him now, that frown, speaking in quiet tones. It would be worse than anything he had ever said.

And here he was, overseeing all of it.

He closed his eyes, not hearing what Yand was saying. It was like the moment had come and wiped away everything. The world whirled, and he stepped over to his chair, feet jerking unnaturally.

he collapsed in it. The man wasn't staring at him from this side, those cold, dead eyes looking straight into his soul.

He felt sick. His stomach rebelled. He had seen death before, but it was peaceful, quiet. Not like this.

Not like this.

"Your highness?"

"Hmm...?" The Duke turned his head, hand trembling. he pulled it back to the armrest of the chair.

"Would you like something to drink? You look a little bit pale."

"Yes. That would be..." Yand walked over to the bar and poured him a glass of the dark red. he took it with hands that betrayed his condition and pulled a deep drink.

It flooded his mouth, threatened to choke him, but he kept it down. Lukewarm, it tasted like ash before it went.

"So, what do we do now?"

"We could try another messenger, but I doubt it'd have any other outcome." Captain Yand returned to his position.

There was a small knock at the door. "It's me."

"Come in." the Duke managed to keep his voice from trembling, but the sheer willpower it took made him take a deep breath.

"I came -- " The eyes of the Overseer fell on the head, cutting him off. He rummaged around in a pocket, finally finding it, and pulled out a handkerchief, which he held daintily to his mouth. "Foul."

"We were just discussing our...guest." Yand said dryly.

"I heard rumors it was Jedediah." He got closer, then squinted. "I couldn't tell if I didn't at least suspect."

"And now we have come to it. Tell me, Overseer, what would you do were you in my shoes?"

"Cut the rations, of course."

"You wouldn't negotiate?"

The Overseer snorted, sending his belly jiggling. "You'd have more luck negotiating with a rock. The Belmarch have their foothold now, the only thing that will drive them from our soil is swords. They don't leave survivors."

"But surely, a noble of my rank would warrant some ransom?" The Duke licked his lips, then remembered his wine. He took another deep gulp.

"No, you don't understand them." The Overseer shook his head. He eyed the wine. The Duke gestured, and he poured himself a glass. "Take it away, no use keeping it in here to smell up the place."

The Duke nodded, and the Overseer summoned a servant. the head was taken out, albeit at arm's length, and with it the smell diminished.

"As I was saying. The Belmarch are raiders, not occupiers. They will try and conquer us and take the land. They don't need gold, they need food and weapons."

"Surely ransom could be paid in steel?" the Duke looked out the window. Sunlight filtered in, and dust motes danced in it. Normally, he would take pleasure in seeing it, but not today.

Not this day.

"They want our blood." The overseer squinted. "Haven't you been taught our history?"

The Duke burned red. "The Duke has taken to sporting like a fish in water," Yand said, stepping in to refill the cup of wine. "His pursuits have been athletic over almost all."

"Ah." The Overseer looked to his right, tapping his chin. "I believe this invitation to negotiate is a trap. They will try to draw us out and strike at us."

"What good would that do?" the Duke asked.

"We would be leaderless, and easier to overpower," Yand said. "Or so they assume. The Belmarch have always been warriors, and see us as weak. A people to be destroyed and murdered."

"They haven't been able to yet. And, with this castle still standing, they won't. They know that, and they'll do everything in their power to get us out of the way," the Overseer said.

"Penned up in here, it doesn't seem like we'd be able to stop them from crossing at all." The Duke turned and stared at the emblem again. He thought about tearing it down, casting it into the fire and seeing it devoured piece by piece.

That would give him some respite of the reminder of what a failure he was. Couldn't even call for help the right way. He shook his head.

"Archers can do some damage, but you're right," Yand conceded. "We aren't in the best position. No one suspected that the Belmarch would be able to send out an army for the rest of the year. We were wrong, and now we have to deal with the consequences."

A sudden weariness overcame him. The lack of sleep, especially the last few nights, and everything that was weighing on him caught up to him. "I grow tired of this talk. We'll ignore the attackers for now. Put more men on the walls though, I want them to think we have more than we really do."

Yand bowed slightly, then saluted. "As you wish, my Lord." He snapped to attention and marched out.

"Leave me," the Duke said, swirling his wine. He took another sip. It was bitter in his mouth, and the aftertaste lingered. It hadn't blunted the headache like he wanted. It hadn't blurred the feelings he had inside either.

He took a bigger swig, then drained the glass. "Leave me."

The Overseer murmured his pleasantries, then departed. The door shut behind him. Duke Hornblood slipped into his chair, feeling the weight of his family upon his shoulders.

The plane scraped down the billet, cutting a whisper thin shaving off. Sam grabbed it and pulled it out of the way. He checked the surface with his hand.

Smooth enough to get away with. "How's this one?"

"Only one way to tell," Ned said. "Archie, do the honors."

Although of average build, Archie held a secret in his frame. He pulled at the ends of the stock, bending it in half.

Sam winced, then looked on. Archie strained, then pushed a little more. Over half a circle's worth, and it still held. "A little stiff."

"I dare not go any thinner." A pile of broken bows had grown in the corner, kept to be reused where they could. Sam thought the best they could get out of them was pegs, but didn't share his misgivings with the others.

"A fresh set of blanks would be helpful," Ned said.

"And where, exactly, do you think we could get those? From the forest we keep hidden out back?"

Kerien sniggered at that, but a quick glance and he was silent and back at work. They hadn't told anyone what they were doing.

Yet.

Sam intended to, when the time was right. He cut in the notches for the bowstring, then rubbed it down with sand to smooth out the worst of the ridges. A few lines of twine around the middle was the best they could do for a hand rest.

A knock on the post. "Who is it?" Sam asked. He hid his bow, then motioned for the others to do the same.

"Master Smith requests your presence, Master Freeman." The voice of Issac, the older of the two blacksmith apprentices, drifted in through the canvas tarps they had put up for privacy. Rain also, but privacy first.

"I'll be there in a minute." The shadow at the door disappeared. Sam doffed his apron and hung up his tools. "Keep working. The more we get done, the better for us all."

"Will we be fletching arrows next?" Kerien asked.

"If need be." Sam ignored the hint of malice in the tone. "Ned's in charge."

He left before Ned could finish his sputtering and protests. The day was nice, not too cool, but with plenty of sunshine.

Wind from the wrong direction brought up the smell of the latrines from the bottom of the walls. It made him wrinkle his nose, but there wasn't anywhere else to put it. At least they had kept it as far away from the well as possible.

A few stretches later, Sam was off. It didn't take long to wander around to the smithy, which still had smoke coming out of his chimney.

Even the Duke had run out of that. It was to be saved for the winter, or used for other things.

Like the bows. If it didn't go well Sam would have some explaining to do. No one authorized use of the wood, and the Overseer had been clear about use of supplies.

Still, it wasn't enough to dampen his spirits, as high as they could be considering the conditions, and he slipped under the roof and into the heat of the smithy.

Greetings were exchanged. Dale put up his tools and apron. "Boys, give us a moment. Take a break up on the wall, if you will."

When the apprentices were gone Dale pulled up a stool for Sam and patted it. "I've done what you asked for. Can't say I'm the best weapon smith around, but it came out decent enough."

He went over to the storage area and pulled out a cloth covered package, the pole Sam had turned sticking out the other end.

A few moments later the cloth was off, and Sam's heart gave a sudden skip of a beat. Dale put it on the table.

It gleamed in the light of the forge, casting rays of yellow and red. The longer he stared, the more it looked like it was on fire.

"Go ahead." Sam reached out at the permission. "I had them polish it to a fine shine."

"You didn't have to do that."

Dale shrugged. "There isn't much else to do. Besides, it takes no fuel."

Like everything else, that too was running out. Wood for the forge, wood for the cook fires. But not enough wood to finish the castle.

"How long do you think it will last?" Sam asked, running his hand along the wooden shaft. He touched the edge of the blade, being careful not to cut himself, then used it to shave off a few hairs on his arm.

They fell, parted as easily as a sharp chisel cuts through pine. He dare not touch the metal again.

"I don't know. Until the end, I expect." Dale crossed his burly arms. "I came here knowing the Belmarch were close. Close enough to kill me."

"You wanted them to come, didn't you?"

"You don't know them like we do, Sam. You haven't seen what they can do." Sam looked up, staring into those haunted eyes. He had always wondered what drove the big man to do what he did.

"Let's hope it doesn't come to that."

"What is your story?" the question took Sam by surprise. He wrapped the spear back up and set it back on the workbench. "We all know you came from somewhere, but never talk about it. Was it the south? Or east?"

"I'd rather not talk about it. That life is gone. That man is dead."

"If that man could help us, maybe it's time to resurrect him." Dale never had been a delicate person. That was something Sam liked about him, how blunt he was. Ore, metal, human. It was all just to hammer into place as needed.

"Thank you for this." Sam wondered why he had done it. The cool, unyielding metal. The warm, hard wood. Why make such a weapon now?

"I hope you'll use it well."

"It isn't for me." Dale eyed him, but could sense the rift that would open if he kept pushing and decided not to ask.

"Consider it a favor for now."

"Am I going to regret it?"

"That depends on how you feel. I haven't decided what to ask in return, but I will ask something."

Sam dipped his head. "Then, whatever it is, when the day comes, I intend to pay it."

20

STICKS AND STONES

Monotony. Day after day, the same. The days grew shorter and the air cooler, and still the Belmarch camped and watched.

Sam almost wished something would happen. They were going to starve them. He wondered what they were thinking, why they hadn't even used the catapult.

It was on the seventh day that he finally found out why.

"They give you seven days to surrender. That's what I heard," Ned told him. They were up on the wall, the brisk autumn breeze chilling him beneath his thin coat.

"What happens if you give up?" Sam saw his breath puff out in white, then caught away. It was early in the morning, and the sun would soon be strong enough to warm them.

Across the field the Belmarch were preparing the catapult for action, or so it appeared. They had found chunks of rock, probably from the quarry, and had stacked up a pile high enough to bring down three castles combined.

"They kill you anyway, but lose less men." Ned was cold, staring at them.

Sam felt the words enter him and dive deep into his soul. What kind of men would do that?

He was starting to suspect he knew. They weren't too different from some men from his past.

And yet, they were. Every day he expected there to be more troops, and every day he was surprised to see about the same number patrolling around the walls.

They were going to try and take them with a force of less than a hundred, and they might do it too.

A few hours after dawn the rocks started to fly. The first one Sam watched get loaded into the catapult, aimed at the gate, then loosed.

It rushed through the air. Men shouted to get down, and it smashed into the wall to the right of the gate.

Sam felt the wall vibrate beneath his feet. His heart was pounding as he watched them load another. The rock they had thrown settled in the field between them.

The cold was forgotten as another came rushing at them. Even though he was well out of the way, he still felt anxious when they came.

The third rock skipped over the top of the wall, almost hitting a man who dove out of the way just in time. It spun and dropped into the courtyard.

Women screamed, clutching at the children and pulling them out of the way. They left everything, the wash, the food, the chores, and ran inside.

Yand was up on the wall now, watching everything transpire. His presence settled the guards and the workers, and he seemed to have no fear of being hit.

"Let them throw their rocks," he said, watching as another bounced off the wall. "These walls are strong, they will hold."

The attack continued through the rest of the day. They were using the leftover rocks from the quarry, of that Sam found out from the conversation of a few masons. They would have more than enough to keep it up.

"How did they get them here?" Sam asked. He took a swig from his water skin, grateful for the warm air.

"I haven't seen a cart or horse anywhere," the man said. It was one of the younger guardsmen, Al, if he remembered right. "Come to think of it, I haven't seen them move them either.

Sam looked harder and saw them moving rocks by hand in the evening twilight. They stopped the attack at night. He guessed it was too dark to see anything.

Before they did, he managed to get a good look at the wall. For the most part, it seemed fine. There were a few chunks missing here and there, and one crenelation now lying in the surrounding field.

Rocks were scattered everywhere, like they didn't know what to aim at. They tried everywhere along the wall, and Sam wondered if they were looking for a weak point.

The gate, however, was unharmed. It had been hit once, but nothing after that. He went down after his watch was fished to check it.

The wood was still solid, still strong. He couldn't see anything wrong with the locking beam, and the braces that held it in place were undisturbed.

"What do you think?" Ned asked, walking up behind him.

"I'm not sure. Why wouldn't they attack the gate?" Ned shrugged at his question.

"They don't want to break it?"

"I thought that would be the point of attacking it."

"They aren't too smart. My guess is that they think it will help them to keep it intact."

Sam realized what they were doing now. "This isn't just an attack to kill us. They want the castle for their own."

Ned cocked his head to one side. "They want to take it over?"

"Yes. They want to use it as a stronghold, an entry point for an invasion, I'm sure of it."

"You should tell the Overseer then. I'm sure he hasn't thought of it, with how un-curious he is."

Sam ran his hand along the rough wood. He had helped build this, it was one of the first tasks he had been assigned when he arrived.

That had been long ago now, it seemed like ages. Despite the change in circumstances, he still felt a distance between him and the Overseer.

"It's just a guess. I don't think it's worth mentioning." Ned looked at him oddly, a cold, searching gaze.

"It wouldn't hurt to tell him."

"Not tonight," Sam demurred. "Maybe in the morning. I feel the day." He yawned, somewhat surprised to feel like he was telling the truth.

How easily lies and deceit seemed to come to him lately.

"Goodnight Ned, I'll see you tomorrow."

"Give it a thought Sam." They shook hands. Ned went to the wall and a long night watch, and Sam went back to the keep.

But it wasn't to sleep, as much as he wished to. Trent was there, waiting for him with practice swords in hand.

Sam took his, after exchanging greetings, and swung it around. "Ready?"

"Yes."

Trent did better than he had in the past, even to the point where Sam had to try and put up a defense to keep away from getting hit by the practice sword.

He was sweating and breathing hard after a few rounds, the chilly night air a welcome refreshment against his skin when they stopped to rest.

The air was clear, but it smelled of refuse and human waste that had built up in the corner near the wall. There wasn't a better place to put it, something they hadn't thought about during the construction of the castle.

Sam caught his breath between bouts, wiping the sweat from his brow. Moonlight glittered against the facets of the wall, splintered by the rough rock surface.

"Has it got any better?" Sam asked when they had finished. "We'll go again tomorrow, I need some rest."

Trent nodded and took the practice sword. He hung around. "You can tell me what's going on."

"What can you do about it?" There was a harshness to his tone, one that surprised Sam.

He was about to reply when he stopped to think about it. What could he do? Ask Bill nicely to stop? Tell the Overseer who already hated him and couldn't stand him? Or go straight to Yand, or even better, the Duke, to put his foot down?

Better to keep his mouth shut than make it worse. But here was Trent, downcast and hating him, and he was right.

Sam searched for the right words, but came up short. "Try your best and that's the best you can do." It was hollow, and he knew it.

He regretted it as soon as it had come out of his mouth.

The chill of the night, now that they weren't moving anymore, had crept into his bones. Winter would come soon, and cold. Cold enough to take away his strength and leave him with nothing.

"May I go now?"

"Tomorrow. We'll meet again tomorrow. Good night, Trent." Trent mumbled something that could have been good night, then was off.

What were they doing to him? Threatening him if he talked to anyone else? He wouldn't put it past Bill, not in the least.

Sam balled up his fists and thrust them down to his sides. He felt the anger, and the thing that he had long since tried to erase at the back of his mind.

It was there, waiting for him to get complacent. To take over when he thought nothing else could make him lose control.

Picturing Bill's face in his mind, he almost did. He looked back to the lean-tos, expecting him.

It was empty. As still as the night. A guard shuffled on the wall above, just out of sight. Here, in the corner of the keep, they were as hidden as anywhere else.

He fought it down. Bit by bit it went away. He tried to relax, to picture himself in the river, drifting and floating with the current instead of fighting against it like the rage he felt.

Deep breaths helped. Slowly, it retreated.

How he longed to be gone from here, from the reminders of a past best left forgotten. He retreated into the keep, out of the wind and warm enough with the bodies of everyone else to banish the autumn chill.

Helpless and a bit hopeless, Sam turned in for the night.

The next day the Belmarchers lobbed a few rocks at the wall, but then stopped before lunch. Sam had watch after lunch and spent the morning with Kerien and Trent in the workshop making more bow, both of whom were off watch.

It didn't go as well as he hoped. The first few bows they made had been fine looking, but after a few shots some of them had cracked and broke.

"Another failure, yet again." Kerien tossed aside his work in progress, too thin to be of any use.

Sam looked up from his, taking light cuts with a chisel around the end where the string would go. He had heard the crack but was too busy to look up then. "Try again."

"I've been trying all day, and all week." Kerien scowled, then crossed his arms. "What good are a few extra bows going to do us, anyway?"

Sam felt along the edge, took another cut, then felt again. It was smooth now, wouldn't cut through the bowstring. He blew off the shavings, then rubbed it with sand. "It isn't what we finish with, it's how we survive. A few extra well placed arrows could help with that."

"So then we should be making arrows."

"If you'd like to try your hand at it, go ahead." A spark of an idea grew inside his mind. "If you're up to it, that is."

"You don't think I can do it." Kerien looked at him with narrow eyes.

"Can you?" Trent asked. His face and voice betrayed a genuine interest, and it was the most alive Sam had seen it in weeks. What scars was the boy hiding underneath that facade?

"I bet I can. It can't be that hard." All of a sudden Kerien's confidence wavered.

"Try splitting first, then the lathe," Sam said. He had seen the young man eying it off to the side.

"Do we have feathers?"

"I saw the children playing with some. Archer took down a few crows flying by." His mouth watered at the thought of the meat, but alas, it was taken into the keep. To the Overseer, no doubt, or the guards if they saw it.

His stomach grumbled remembering the stuffed goose they would have at the new year back home. Moist, succulent, bursting with flavor and covered with dried berries saved from the last summer harvests and piping hot potatoes covered in butter.

Sam ground down on his teeth, banishing the thought. With the reduced rations everyone was hungry, and the reminder made him conscious of the other's need too.

"There's some twine in the supplies. You might be able to use it to tie them on."

"I'm going to do it. You'll see." Sam was glad to hear it. There was something for him to do, and less complaining too. It had started to grate on him, and he knew it bothered the others.

But with so little work and so much anticipation of attack, how else was Kerien supposed to feel?

Kerien took up a stick long enough to get a few arrows out of, then cut it to length. Sam considered asking Dale to make a few arrowheads, then pulled himself back.

There wasn't any guarantee this was going to work. They weren't fetchers and bowyers, they were carpenters.

But Kerien had taken up the challenge, and even Sam perked up at the thought. He didn't know who kept count of the arrows, but he doubted they had enough to fend off an army.

And adding more to that number couldn't hurt any.

Sam watched and looked on as Kerien split the log in half, then halves again. Soon he had a pile of shafts, not quite ready to be made into arrows.

Somehow, just having them lifted Sam's spirits. Perhaps, just maybe, they could find a way out of this siege if they worked together.

21

A Meeting in the Night

The arrows turned out to be easier to make than he thought. Soon they had a bundle of crow-feather attached headless arrows waiting for something to attach to the top.

"Impressive," Ned said, fingering one. He pulled on the feather to see how well it was attached. It held, even with some substantial force. "How many do you think we will need?"

"Far too many for us to make. I overheard some guards talking about how they feared they would run out and there would be nothing left to stop the Belmarch." Sam sighted down one. There was a slight bend, but not too much.

"I've got to go on watch, will you keep working on these?" Sam put the arrow back in the pile. "And don't spread the word. I've asked Kerien not to as well..."

"Say no more." Ned clapped a hand on his back. "We'll take care of what we can."

Sam stroked his beard, now full and long, and thought about a good shave with warm water. How the blade would part the hairs and leave his chin cool, feeling the breeze once again.

The same breeze blew through the workshop, and he was suddenly grateful for the beard again. "Winter's coming too fast."

"We'll manage." Sam didn't see how, with the weak coats and poor coverings they had and no way to get more.

"Sam Freeman," said a voice from behind him. Sam turned.

"What is it?"

"Will you come with me, please?" There wasn't much confidence in his voice, and after Sam exchanged a glance with Ned, turned and followed.

"What is this about?"

"They need to see you."

"Who?" The guard pursed his lips, but kept on walking. A dozen reasons rushed through his head, but Sam pushed them all away.

Better to find out than to make it worse than it had to be.

"I'll find out then." Sam followed the man through the keep and down the side passage to a familiar door.

The guard knocked once, and a voice bade them enter.

Inside was like a different world, with the scent of filth and the outside replaced with rug and wine. The Duke sat in his chair, the imposing crest above his head hanging as a constant reminder of who was in charge.

The guard shoved him forward into the room and Sam stumbled. He caught himself and bowed before the Duke.

Captain Yand was in the corner of the room, standing next to an empty fireplace.

"Sam, may I call you Sam?" The Duke was smiling, his face young and handsome, but strained. These past few weeks had not been easy on him, and it showed.

"Certainly, Sire."

"Captain Yand told me of your quick thinking and you action that led to the repulsion of the Belmarchers."

"It was nothing that any other would have done." Sam bowed his head and dropped his gaze to the floor. Surely there was something else to this summons. That was days, weeks ago. Why bring it up now?

"You showed real courage, if what I hear is true. However..." The Duke tapped on his desk. "You seem to be holding something back, not giving your all, should we say?"

Sam's mouth dried up. How much did he know?

"I want to change that, and I'll need your help. Would you care for some wine?" The Duke nodded and a servant poured a glass. With a quick movement across the room, it was offered and placed in Sam's hand.

He stared at it. How long had it been since he had a good glass of wine? Before he came here, of that he was certain.

It was dark red and smelled wonderful. He caught hints of honey in with the grape, fermented at the peak of the harvest with the juice as plentiful as it could be.

What was happening? Why was he being called here?

"May I speak freely?" Sam asked.

"Go ahead."

"What is it you want of me?"

"What is it I want?" The Duke stood up. He was in full regalia, including a cape. "I want from you what I want from every one of my subjects. To obey my commands and provide the very best they can."

"I understand, Sire. That I have done since the moment I arrived here."

"I've been told of your handiwork, but there are other talents that you have that you have been hiding, isn't that right?"

Sam didn't know what to say. It wasn't right, not anymore. But he couldn't say that, not after training Trent. There would be no truth in it.

He was caught, like a fish in a barrel. Now all they had to do was throw in the spear and run him through.

"Is there anything you would like to share with us?" Yand asked, moving away from the fireplace and circling Sam.

Sam took a drink of the wine, and it flowed to the back of his throat. It was good, some of the best he'd ever tasted. Mellow and smooth, with a hint of oak and an aftertaste of honey just like it smelled.

"We are in a siege, with the chances of us walking away low," Yand said. He went behind the desk and stood next to the Duke. "Anything that could help would be your responsibility to provide."

"He speaks the truth," the Duke said.

"I swore off that life a long time ago," Sam managed to choke out, his voice cracking. "I'm afraid I'm of no use."

"At least train the men, give them a fighting chance."

Sam shook his head. "I was never that good. Never at the level you are, Captain."

"You don't seem to see the seriousness of the situation." Sam raised his gaze and locked eyes with the Duke. "This isn't a game that you can walk away from if the turn doesn't go your way. There are men out here that need you, that rely on you to survive. Are you just going to walk away from them like they don't exist?"

"I'll do everything I can to help them." Sam unclenched his fist. "Everything I can, not everything you ask." He set the glass of wine down. It didn't feel right with what everyone else had to eat and drink.

Here he was, warm and enjoying something he hadn't had in months, and everyone else was out in the cold, shivering. They were on the walls, they were keeping watch.

Something stirred within him, itching to break free. The thing he feared the most. Coiled, lying in wait. They were calling to it, they were trying to wake it up.

And he had to keep it asleep.

"I can build for you. Give me the men and we'll make something they'll regret invading every step they take within these walls." Sam looked up. The Duke's eyes were widened, and his mouth parted slightly. Captain Yand stared at him. "I can't fight for you, but I can do this."

Duke Hornblood looked to Yand, who came up beside him. The two talked in hushed tones, too soft for him to hear. Yand frowned, but turned to Sam.

"What did you have in mind?"

The Overseer was brought into the room, summoned by a servant, and despite his hesitancy, they planned.

It took hours, poring over the rough maps and schematics of the castle. Sam mustered all his knowledge, all his experience, but still could only think of things to build.

He would need the others to put the plan into action. And one of those was Bill.

"It would be better if you approached Bill," Sam said, turning to Overseer Rhys to broach the topic. He had remained cool toward him the whole time, only responding to Yand and the Duke.

"I suggest if you need something done about your problems, you handle it yourself." The Overseer looked down his nose at him, voice filled with ice.

Sam took a deep breath. There was no sense in getting mad at a man who could throw you in chains at the second he was provoked. He doubted even the Duke would try to contradict an order like that. "I understand, sir. Is there anything you suggest I do to... repair our relationship?"

"I suggest you own up for your past mistakes. You cost this project time and resources, and money, by your inability to plan ahead and complete what you were responsible for. We never had a problem when Luca was in charge."

He wanted to remind the Overseer they had about four more carpenters before they were all killed by the Rotting Sickness, but that too would have helped nothing.

"I've taken full accountability for when we have failed, but I'll not take that responsibility for someone else."

"Do you mean to call me a liar?" The Overseer's eyes were bulging now, his great cheeks puffed up with air. Hot air.

"Gentlemen," Yand warned. His voice carried the weight of command with it, and what he could do to back it up. "Why don't we call it a night and meet in the morning? I could use a good night's sleep."

"Good idea," the Duke said, cutting off the Overseer. "Sam, please leave us."

Sam stood and saluted, then walked for the door. He hazarded one last glance in the room. The Overseer was seething, and his heart dropped, but was that a hint of a smile on Yand's face?

He shut the door behind him. His mind was buzzing from the night and the ideas with even more percolating up.

He thought about going to sleep, but then realized he would be up in another hour or so for watch anyway, and wandered out of the keep and into the courtyard.

The night was calm, the sentries on the wall walking a now well-known route around the perimeter. Sam went to the workshop and looked over the supplies, running his hand over the raw wood to feel its roughness.

His mind wandered to the spear hidden in the corner of the workshop, covered in clutter and not forgotten. Why had he hidden it there, amongst broken projects and broken tools?

And what was it for, if not to give to one of the others. It would be a powerful weapon in Captain Yand's hands, and the other guards would benefit from it as well.

But he hadn't given it to them. Not when it was finished, not days after. He had hidden it here.

For what purpose? Sam brooded on it, couldn't escape it, until the watch bell rang and it was his time to go back up onto the wall.

Throughout the night, as his energy drained away and frustration and exhaustion started to take him, Sam wondered and fought himself.

"What do you think?" The Duke rubbed his temples, the weight settling there. It helped, a little.

"A man who did what he did is either a fool or brave. Like I said before, he is no fool." A servant took away the glasses to wash. Duke Hornblood looked to the fireplace, wishing they had enough wood to make it burn cheerfully. The stone walls sucked the heat from the room in the night, robbing him of the little comfort he had left. Even the tapestries didn't help much.

"I often wonder if I'll ever live up to the expectations of my father, let alone the rest of the family." The words felt strange, but he needed to speak them. There was no one else to share them with, not now. He had no peers in this place. He was utterly and irrefutably alone.

Yand listened and kept his face blank. He had always been respectful that way, never giving any indication of what Duke Hornblood had meant to him.

"I thought this...assignment was going to be the one that finally let him see that his son wasn't a worthless dandy." He smiled ruefully, and stared up at the crest. The urge to tear it down was even stronger now, and he clasped his hands behind him, fingernails digging painfully into his skin.

It was a feeling, though. One not washed in wine or liquor.

"You are no dandy, and you are far from worthless."

"Kind words, Yand, but I'm afraid you aren't the liar you make out to be." He could see it on his face, plastered all over it. Empty words. Like his empty name. "Now I'm afraid I'll always be the son who lost the castle before it was even finished."

He couldn't stand it anymore and swept up the glass, downing the wine in one long gulp. "I'd like to be alone now."

Yand snapped to attention, saluted, and was out the door in a second, leaving the Duke to nurse his cups in the dying candlelight.

22

KEEP YOUR ENEMIES CLOSE

The arrows clattered onto the table. "Can you help us out with these?"

Dale picked up the top arrow, examining the end of it. "Looks like it isn't going to work very well." He held up the headless end.

"Funny." Sam crossed his arms. Dale was grinning from ear to ear and holding in great guffaws. "You didn't answer my question, though."

"I can help. We've got the iron, but I'm worried about the fuel."

"What do you have to do besides this?"

Dale shook his head, smile fading away. "The Duke has me making swords. I'm not a weapon smith, and the spear was hard enough, but I've only been able to make three in the last week."

"Three is better than nothing." The smoke of the forge, smaller than usual but still billowing, drifted through the air. Drips of water fell from the eaves, plopping down into the puddles fresh from the rain.

"Has Bill been by here?" He didn't know why it popped into his brain, but it was out before Dale could answer his question. That made the last of his smile disappear.

"I try to make it clear this isn't a good place for him. He hasn't been by in some time." He dropped the headless arrow back into the stack. "I'll see what we can do about these, in between swords. Arrows would be better anyway."

"I don't know which was better; Bill with all the ale he could drink, or Bill with none of it."

"He's a vicious one. Wiry, but strong. The drink softened him, if he was in the right mood." The thought of it made Sam remember times he wasn't in the right mood.

"I need a way to get him to come around to me."

Dale snorted. "Easier to get a mule to follow your commands, without a thick stick for prodding."

"I'm at an impasse. I don't know how to handle him and neither does anyone else."

"He's afraid of you."

Sam furrowed his brow. "Bill isn't afraid of me. He's afraid of you, not me."

"Not in the same way. He's afraid of me because of these." Dale held up a bulky arm. "There's something else in you that makes him afraid."

Afraid? Of me? He thought back on their interactions about the emotions Bill displayed. He thought it had been disgust, jealousy maybe. Not that he had anything to be jealous of. *But fear?*

Never.

"If he was afraid of me, he wouldn't be doing what he is to Trent."

"I've heard the rumors. Are they true?" Sam nodded. Dale rubbed his chin, his lips tightening. "What a fool. You have your work cut out for you then, and I'm not sure I'll be of much use."

"Well, if you can think of anything I'll be all ears." Sam looked out to the courtyard. "Rain's let up, I need to go." A stone smashed into the wall, and Sam sighed. "They've started again."

"Better get to it." They clasped hands, then Sam turned.

It was time to pay a visit, one he had been putting off for days.

The shack was bigger than the others, made with the best stones and solid. No wind would get through those walls, only the roof was a weak point.

Sam stood for a second, gathering his wits, and knocked. Shuffling from inside, then it opened.

A whiff of something strange came out of the open crack. Sam couldn't put a finger on what it was, but it wasn't unpleasant.

"What do you want? Come to beg for your apprentice?"

"I came to talk, nothing more."

Bill eyed him. He was leaner than he had been, not gaunt, but wiry. It was in his cheeks.

The shack was well furnished, with a bed and a table, and even two chairs. How he had found these, Sam was baffled. Bill was nothing if not resourceful.

"Come in." Bill opened the door. He was alone, for once.

"Thank you." *Now, how to start?* Bill took a seat, but didn't offer him one. "How long do you think we'll last, divided like we are?"

His eyes narrowed. *Good, he was thinking for once.* That was unkind, but Sam felt some unhealthy satisfaction in the thought.

"I aim to stay alive for a few more decades or so." Bill put a hand on the table, but kept the other one beneath it. Sam took note of it.

"May I?" Sam gestured to the open chair. Standing above would be no use, they needed to be on the same level, see eye to eye. Bill nodded after a pregnant pause. Just enough to be impolite. "I know we've had our differences, and I haven't always taken the time to find out why. I want to change that now."

"Very noble of you." It was dripping with sarcasm.

Sam took a seat, put both hands palm up on the table. "As a gesture of goodwill, I will start by admitting something you've suspected but haven't been able to confirm."

Bill leaned in, ever so slightly, but his lips stayed tight.

"With your permission, of course," Sam said.

"Go on."

"I'm not from Chathem. I can pass off easily enough, I have some distant blood on one side of my family, but my homeland is Unarcia."

"I suspected you weren't from around here. Lying about your heritage, what else have you been hiding?"

"Never lied about it, and you know it. Refusing to talk about it I can be accused of, of that I'll admit, and evading any question on the subject. That is fair, but not lying."

"I don't see the distinction."

"You might not," Sam said. "I left a life behind, one I had grown tired of after years. I came to Chathem to make a new life for myself and escape war and death." Flashes of battle, and it pained him to remember. Sam shut his eyes and took a deep breath, banishing it to the far reaches of his mind.

"Why did you run? Cowardice?" There was always a dig, a little knife in the words. He knew it was to set him off guard, to roil his emotions. It was working, but Sam had to stop it.

What had Ned said? That we all have things we're running from. Something changed in Sam's mind, he realized that Bill would be the same.

What was he running from? What life had he left behind? That explained the rough words, the sharp jabs.

Knowing that changed everything. The creases in Bill's eyes didn't mean he was angry with Sam, he was angry with himself.

Sam was the conduit, Sam was the element that brought it out.

"You run from your past, just as fast as I run from mine." Bill's eyes widened, just a hair. His lips snapped shut. "You've done violence, haven't you?"

"You don't know anything about me," Bill growled, setting his head down.

"Then tell me. What am I missing? Were you a brigand, a thief perhaps?" A reaction rippled across Bill's face. *So that was it.* "You've killed, I can see it in your eyes. It pains you."

Bill's mouth wriggled and fought. It opened, then closed again.

"Whatever you've done, I don't care." There was a power in knowing. "You may kill again, for a good cause. You might do violence again, for the weak and helpless. You might change." Were those words for Bill?

He looked away. "You don't know what kind of life I've live," Bill said. The fight had gone out of his tone. It was warm in the room, from their bodies and the heat of the sun warming the stone walls. The table was smooth from years of use.

"Perhaps we have a common enemy, one willing to cut off our heads and throw them over walls without blinking an eye." Sam pressed, leaning forward. "Perhaps we've known each other a few years, and that we have more in common than we think. Perhaps we learn to set aside our differences and fight together."

"I don't trust that you'd fight. You'd turn and run at the first sign of trouble."

"You know that's not true, and I don't think you would either." Bill's shoulders drooped. "I've killed men too, Bill." His eyes snapped to Sam's. "I can't change that fact, and it haunts me to this day."

The eyes. Remembering the eyes haunted him. The fear, the hate, the terror. Seeing the life drain out of them like water from a cracked jug.

It came over him now, caressing the thing deep inside. For there was another fear, another thing he was hiding. That was a secret he could tell no man.

It would go with him to his grave.

Bill's eyes showed his emotions, what he was thinking. Every flicker, every blink. Sam could read it all, could feel it just as bill felt.

"I...I've done things. I'm not proud of them."

"Look at what you've built here. Great walls that keep us safe, a castle to protect us from enemies. That is no mean feat, not done of a little man."

"I'd like you to leave now." Bill cast his gaze to the ground. Outside, a bird chirped. Sam's heart sank. He had been so close. He tried to think of words that would finish what he started. None came.

There would be no reconciliation, no putting away of things better left behind.

Sam stood. "I'll leave, but just remember what I said."

Bill said nothing. Didn't move, didn't even look at Sam.

There was nothing left to say. Sam turned and left, shutting the door on Bill. He wondered, as he walked away, if it was forever.

Stone scraped on iron. Again and again, Sam dragged the chisel across the sharpening stone. The pungent oil, soaked into the stone, kept the temper of the chisel as he cut fine shavings away from the blade.

He thought as he sharpened, letting his mind wander and his hands work free of thought. Scrape. The lantern shivered, caught by a gust of wind blowing through the workshop.

Scrape. The iron was cold in his hands. Scrape. *What to do?*

The first lesson he had learned as an apprentice was to sharpen the tools. Hour after hour, he sat at the sharpening stone. He sharpened until his hands blistered and his fingers stung, stained black from the iron.

He had taken to it surprisingly well, making his master pleased. He didn't tell him why at the time, but these weren't the only blades he had sharpened.

Sam tested the bevel. Flat, straight. Not like the situation he was in right now. If only things would be so easy as this in real life.

He looked to the sky then, the clouds of a fall rain rumbling on the horizon. There was an electricity in the air, sparks from the foretelling of lightning, and the air was thick with the smell of rain.

Back to the spear. It haunted him, followed him.

He had no wish to use that blade, to bring out the thing inside him, but what choice did he have?

Sam sucked in a breath, then let it out. "Control yourself, control the blade." That was the second lesson his master had taught him. He hadn't forgotten it all these years later.

He could burn it. Cast it into the fire and let his desires be devoured once and for all. Sam shook his head. *It would do no good, it would still follow me.*

That only left one option. To use it.

The chisel was sharp now, and a few tests on the end grain of an old chunk of gnarly oak yielded clean, fresh shavings and no tear out.

He returned the chisel to the leather bundle, joining its brothers all in a row. Each one was razor sharp, ready for use.

To build. That was who he was now. A creator, not a destroyer. He was here to build, to make, to improve.

So why did it have to be so hard? He tied the smooth, leather thong that captured the roll and set the tools back beneath the bench.

There was no stalling now. Thunder rolled through the workshop, the first drops falling on the thatch roof and dust outside. They puffed up small clouds of dust that were driven down by the next drop.

Sam looked back and walked out into the rain, letting the cold pinpricks fall on his head and shoulders.

The warning bell rang out, cries accompanying it. They were attacking again.

23

SURPRISES AT THE GATE

Men rushed to the gate, and Sam was not far behind. His heart was racing, and he took a bow from the stack, noting it was one of theirs. How had it gotten here?

"How long?" he asked, crouching down beside Ned. A crash of stone slammed into the wall.

"Not long." He winced as, a few seconds later, an arrow clattered against the wall. Sam took a quick peek as Ned nocked an arrow.

They were assembled into rows, and Sam wasn't sure it was the same amount. Had they had reinforcements arrive?

"Who saw them?"

"The western watch." Sam handed him another arrow. The feathers brushed his hands. Ned stood up and pulled back. A few seconds later, he dropped back down. "Too far."

"On the eastern flank!" A guard shouted out from that side. "Ladders are coming."

Another rock smashed into the wall, breaking off a crenelation and falling into the courtyard with a smash.

The sun was out, and the day was warm. The chill of the morning was still in the stone, though, and it bit his unprotected hands.

They were prepared this time, with long sticks that mirrored his first set. They could try and use the ladders again, but it wouldn't turn out well for them.

Sam doubted they would, or that if they did, it was the only thing they would do. Whatever the Belmarchers had done in the past, they learned well.

They were covering their advance with arrows, poorly placed but enough to make the guards on the wall duck down and keep their cover.

It was stupid. They had a better firing position from up here, but it wasn't his place to try and urge them to fight.

Deep inside the thing was growling, forcing him to act. He fought desperately to keep it calm. Sam squeezed his eyes shut.

The sound of the enemy approaching broke through his defenses. There was an energy in the air. This wasn't a feint, a move designed to distract them and wear them down. Hour after hour could pass that way.

This was something entirely altogether different.

"How long do you think it will take for them to retreat again?" Kerien ran up, ducking down behind him. Sam looked him in the eye.

"They won't."

Kerien's grin faded, but Sam couldn't bear to see it. He returned his gaze to the field.

He saw it before the others. Before he heard the creak of the wheels, before he smelled the fresh pine and oak it was made from.

"Battering ram!" The cry went out up and down the wall, punctuated by another rock from the catapult.

"That won't work, will it?" Kerien peered over the wall, then looked back to Sam and Ned. "Will it?"

They were firing the catapult strategically, aiming at the largest clusters of men on the walls. "They've been practicing on us."

That was what all those rocks were for, now scattered throughout the fields of the walls.

"Incoming," Ned said. They ducked down, the rock smashing against the wall just below them. It shuddered beneath their feet, and the crenelation shifted perceptibly.

"Spread out," Sam said.

The guardsmen were up on the wall in force now, and each of the squad leaders was assembling their men at the assigned locations. Ned and Kerien were pulled away, leaving Sam with the rest of his squad.

"Hold your arrows," Matthew said. He was shaking, not cut out for this level of fighting. "Orders are to fire when given the command." His voice was filled with uncertainty, but Sam stood behind him.

"When given the order, make it count." Matthew looked relieved, almost glad. Sam felt sorry for him and wondered if he would live the rest of the day.

He had made it this far, there was always hope. He seemed to be a firm guard on his own, it was the leadership that changed him.

Even now, he looked back at Yand in the guardhouse atop the gate, who was busy giving orders and stoking the fires.

The battering ram was trundling up the road. Few rocks were blocking its way, and the covered roof was protecting the enemy pushing it.

It looked wet. Sam frowned. They had soaked it in water, of that he was sure. Clever. That would stop fire from reaching it.

He glanced at the oak.

It was only a matter of time now. The creak of the wheels rose from its steady progress, men chanting and keeping time within. He couldn't make out their words and didn't want to.

"We need to brace the gate." Sam turned to Matthew. "They'll break it down if we don't."

"My orders were to the wall, as are yours." Fool of a man, choosing this moment to grow a spine.

He needed more time. All the plans, if they got it, it would be for nothing. "Let me talk to Captain Yand."

"Ladders!" The warning run out on their side.

"Repel invaders," Matthew said, turning to the wall. "Archers ready."

"Fire volley!" The order came from the gatehouse, ringing out clear. Guards were yelling to target the battering ram, but it was completely protected.

There was nothing to aim at, nothing to hit.

Sam ran up the line, distributing arrows to the waiting men. They shot at the ladder carriers and made them regret not moving fast enough.

But enemy archers were giving back almost as much in return. A man cried out, pulling back with an arrow in his shoulder.

Another toppled back, falling over with an arrow in his eye. Sam helped the wounded, bandaging them when he could and helping them down to the courtyard below where women waited to care for them when he couldn't.

"Take care of him," Sam said, handing off a young mason to Martha. She nodded and started to work, breaking off the arrow shaft. The man screamed in pain.

Sam looked up at the guardhouse, then at the gate. The stairs were right there, less than a few feet from his own squad. It would just take a few seconds, that was it.

Then, a pounding on the gate made his mind for him. The gate shook, dust falling from the top, reverberating in the castle courtyard.

Sam turned and sprinted to the wooden stockpile, urging anyone he could see to help him. The men were on the walls, fighting and dying now. They tried to push away the ladders, but they kept coming. Sam struggled to pick up the largest beams still in the stockpile, bellowing for help.

No one came from the walls, but there were women and children flowing from the keep. They helped him, struggling to pick it up, but with enough of them and Sam's direction, they were able to drag it across the courtyard.

He set the end of it as high as he could get it. A few men had come down from the wall and were helping now. The gate was buckling, the locking bar cracking and bending dangerously.

He could feel it cracking, could hear the sound and it sent dread deep inside with every click and scratch.

"Brace, there." They set the other end in the mud. Kerien was there, beside him now. "Get a hammer and nails. And you, get more wood."

They pushed one end into the ground deeper, and the methodical pounding continued.

He was breathing hard, the strain of pulling the wood across the yard catching up to him. Blood mixed with the smell of dust and ash, faint but still there. He felt sick, but there was nothing else he could do.

That's not true, is it?

The image of the spear came to mind, but Kerien was there with the hammer and nails. He set a chunk of wood above the beam, hammering it into place.

Each hit from the battering ram drove the new brace deeper. More wood came, more beams to brace. The iron sounded like it was giving way.

The tip of the battering ram broke through, splintering the gate.

"Archer, we need archers down here!" Sam yelled. It was confusion, men were everywhere. The hole grew, the pointed end of the ram widening it.

There were men on the other side, and bowmen of their own. An arrow sailed past Sam's head, stinging his scalp. He hardly felt anything but the blood running down his cheek.

A few bows were there now, and an exchange took place. Water splashed down from above, the murder holes no doubt, but the roof of the ram meant it only trickled under the gate and underfoot, making a dirty scene even worse.

Sam slipped on it, falling against the door. A splinter drove into his hand, and he pulled it out and threw it away.

It would hurt in a few minutes, but he had to keep going. He hammered another brace home. Sweat mixed with the blood, stinging his head with the salt. He wiped it away, but it only made the wound worse.

"Hold fast." Yand was there now, urging the men back into position even as the arrows flew. Another beam went up, driven into the ground.

The ram started again, slamming against the hole to widen it.

It forced Sam back, barely keeping his footing. He came back to the door just as it slammed again, crunching the thick oak and splintering it.

Bows twanged and arrows flew. The hole was noticeable, wide enough to get a man through, but only if they forced it.

"Wood, hand me wood." Sam motioned to Kerien, pointing to the hole. His lungs burned and ached. Something was burning on the other side, sending billows of acrid black smoke through the hole.

Kerien saw and disappeared. The braces were moving, but still holding. They bent with each blow, and casualties were building up.

However, the defenders were keeping up a steady rhythm of arrow fire into the hole. The ram creaked less, the shudders were fewer. For a moment Sam started to hope.

Then he saw the attackers on the walls. They were coming up ladders and fighting on the ramparts.

And these men were fighters. Not like the tradesmen that faced them with minimal training and poor weaponry.

"They're coming up the west side," Sam said, and pointed. Yand followed his direction, frowning.

"You, you, stay here. Keep up a steady fire and feed them arrows until they burst. Everyone else with me."

Yand turned and led the force up the wall, leaving just two men to defend against the battering ram party.

Kerien was back, carrying the thickest planks they had. With a quick duck and few dodges, he was on the other side, sliding the first across the gap.

The archers joined them, dropping their bows to pick up braces. Sam hammered the braces into place just as the battering ram hit them.

They bowed dangerously, but the plank stood up to it. He had a moment of sadness, that would have been a good, sturdy table top, before he finished the last nails.

Frustration welled up inside him. It was the final straw. A symbol of what had come, a relic of his past.

All the hours he had put into this place. The heartache, the late nights. The friendships he had developed, and the grief of those friends gone just as easily as they had come.

He had no need to keep the beast down now. It was asleep, just like his future would be.

"Sam?" Kerien was beside him. "You're hurt." He was troubled, looking at his head.

"This?" Sam touched his head, it came away bloody. It stung. "It isn't bad."

They were still pounding on the gate, although it was weak. They must have lost men, too many to replace. Trying an attack from all directions had been too much.

But, judging from the fighting on the walls, it had been a worthwhile distraction. Yand was up there, fighting and killing with ease and skill Sam hadn't seen in years.

His sword seemed to be lightning, flashing from one man to the next. None could stand against him, and it gave him hope that they could fight this back, survive another day.

One by one the ladders were pushed off the western wall. One by one, the attackers fell to the onslaught of the hulking fighter within the walls of the castle.

Heat flowed through the cracks and splinters of the massive oak gate. Sam leaned against it, watching the flickers of fire come through.

Captain Yand had dispatched the last attacker, his body slumping against the rock. He sheathed his sword as Sam caught his breath.

Yand took up a stick, and with another, pushed at the ladder. It fell back, but then so did Yand, clutching at his face.

Sam watched in horror as Captain Yand slipped on the rock and tumbled into the courtyard below.

24

DEATH OF A GIANT

His heart beat in his throat. Sam willed Yand to get up, but he knew he wouldn't.

The sounds of battle continued around him, but it seemed to fade as he rushed over to the body.

Life had drained from him, the eyes locked in surprise with an arrow sticking out from his neck. Others were there beside him. Hands sought a heartbeat, a breath of air, something.

Martha closed his eyes with a bloody hand. "There is nothing we can do for him."

Finality.

Yand had been taken to oblivion, left them here to experience death and destruction.

Sam closed his eyes. It wasn't his fault, he didn't decide to leave them, but the end result was still the same.

They were left without a leader, without a fighter. Where was the Duke? Holed up in the keep while everyone else fought? Away from the stench of battle, the smell of the dead. Away from the blood and gore that came so easily to war.

Away from everything he had tried to run away from, and failed.

Sam rocked back on his heels. His eyes opened. they were taking the body away now, carrying it back to the keep with the others.

Men still fought on the wall. Arrows were loosed, ladders were pushed. They still came on, relentlessly.

Sam felt like there was a weight on his chest, pressing against him. He gasped. Too little air, he had to breathe.

When he did, he almost threw up from the smell. Men were screaming, dying. Attacker, defender, it didn't matter.

He should have left long ago, when Luca died. How could he not see it?

He knew this could happen. Why had he still chosen to come?

He sat down, ready to go where he needed. But where was that? Not here. He had been ineffective, walked right back into the life he hated.

Someone was calling his name. He looked up at the wall. Ned was shooting his bow, a determined look on his face.

Trent. Where was he? He had forgotten all about him. The west wall. He had been at the heart of the fighting, where Yand had died.

Scanning the ramparts, Sam saw no hint of his apprentice.

Heart sinking, he leaned back on his knees. Another failure in a long line of them.

The sounds of battle faded, and Sam slipped into his own mind.

Flashes of the past materialized, then decayed away, one after the other. Faster than the speed of light, yet as slow as anything he had experienced before.

This would be his grave, his death knell. It would ring out through the ages to mark an insignificant, unknown man who made nothing of a mark on the world.

All his work would be destroyed, cast aside, corrupted. The wood, the stone, the rock. Torn down piece by piece.

He took a deep breath.

There was no point. The Belmarchers would get in, they would fight, and they would kill all of them. The women, the children. Everyone.

He was dead. What good would it do to fight now?

Bill was walking toward him. For what reason, Sam knew not. He stopped in front of him, obscuring his view of the fighting.

There was a strange look in Bill's eyes. Hatred, disgust, rage perhaps?

"You sit there in the dust when others fight?"

The words cut deep, deep into the very heart of him. But Sam knew it was no use arguing with him. Trent was right, Bill was right. He was a coward.

And now he would meet his end, the same way.

"I thought better of you." The words surprised him, shocking Sam out of his thoughts.

"Why?"

"You never struck me as the cowardly type." Sam's eyes opened wide at that. "Pompous, self-righteous, yes. But not a coward."

Anger struck him, the thing deep inside stirring for the first time in hours.

Bill turned. "Stay there in the dirt where you belong. Humbled, waiting for the axe to fall." He looked back at him over his shoulder. "As for the rest of us, we will fight without you. Trent will fight." He flung his head to the east wall.

Trent was there, sword flashing in the sunlight. Ladders stuck up over the wall, but he was leading the charge. Trent, barely a man.

And here he was, wallowing in the dirt like a pig. Sam looked down at his bloodstained hands. Would they ever be clean again?

"Goodbye Sam. You've been chained by your own thoughts for far too long. I hope death frees you of them," Bill said, and then walked away.

Emotions raged through Sam. Anger at being rebuked by the very man who had the least standing to do it, but being right about it. Pride at seeing Trent fighting so hard and so well. Fear, at feeling the old thing coming back to life again, itching to be released.

His mouth was dry, his lips cracked as he opened it. Licking his lips, he got to his feet. His legs trembled from the events of the day. He was so tired. "I'll not stand by and have you take what little honor I had."

Bill stopped.

"You don't know what I've done, what I have tried to forget." Sam's eyes watered at the memories.

"We've all done things we've regretted. Didn't you know that, Sam Freeman?" Bill walked away, a smile playing on his lips.

For the first time in years, a flame of hope flickered within him. How could he let these people die when he had the ability to at least fight to stop it?

He gnashed his teeth and turned, taking the first step across the courtyard. Men died, falling from the walls. Another step. Women tore at their clothes, using them as bandages to stop bleeding. Another step.

Children cried, others faced it stern faced and stubborn. Another step. The thing within him woke up, and he held its leash tight.

Never again.

His feet knew the path, and his hands reached under the cloth, closing around the handle of the spear.

He drew it out and turned back to the wall, ready to face the enemy.

25

ONE BY ONE

For the first time in years Sam cast an eye across the battlefield and analyzed it. Gone were the doubts, banished to the farthest reaches of his mind.

Now was the time to act.

The eastern and southern walls were taking the most in the attack. Somehow, after the push from Yand, the western wall seemed under control.

But the rest of the castle was in utter chaos. Men were running, fighting, retreating without any rhyme or reason.

Sam knew what he had to do. He gripped the warm shaft of the spear and sprinted to the southern wall.

The longest of all the defenses, it continued to be bombarded by rocks through from the catapult. Ned was up there, with Archie by his side, and the rest of two squads.

Smoke rose from the guardhouse above the gate. He would be surprised if anyone was still up there. The gate was still holding, even though flames licked at it.

Sam grabbed hold of the shirt of a boy running by. Scrawny, with eyes darting like a lizard, he knelt down next to him.

"Joseph, do you remember me?" The boy nodded, fear filling his eyes. "I'm not going to hurt you, but those men are. Will you do me a favor?"

"My mom told me to hide in the keep."

"And she's a good woman. Will you go get her and get as many as you can to get buckets and anything else that can hold water?" The boy was still frightened. "I won't say anything about where I met you, deal?"

"Where should we take them?" His voice was cracked with fear, but it held together.

"Captain Yand needs you to fill them and take them to the guardhouse above the gate. You're a very brave young man. I know you'll do well." The eyes calmed, and Sam let him go. He stood on his own feet, not yielding an inch. "Go now, as quick as a rabbit."

The boy took off, headed for the keep. Sam wasn't sure it would work, or that anyone would listen to the young boy, but they needed every fighting age man on the wall.

Trent was holding his own, even rallying the rest of his squad. They were pushing back the ladders, keeping the rest of the attackers at bay.

Another wave of pride washed over him, glad that the young man had taken so well to swordplay. Even though he was rusty, it had never been his strong suit.

The tip of the spear glinted in the sunlight. The lance, on the other hand...

It felt good to hold in his hands. This time, he was less ashamed of it. These were good, honest men and women. They deserved lives free of murder and fear, to live out a simple life in service to their families.

He wanted them to eat, to be loved, to laugh again. The castle had been filled with too many gaunt faces, too much sorrow, for too long.

An inkling of a plan started to form in his mind. It was a wild shot, but he wasn't sure they had any other options.

Fire and water. Balance, and enemies.

"Ned!" Sam reached the bottom of the stairs and started to take them two at a time. His legs and lungs protested, but he ignored them.

Ned's face appeared above him. He was blood-stained and exhausted. One of his arms was cut, and he was favoring his left leg.

"We can't hold them off much longer."

"I know it. You've done well." He reached him, looking down the lines of men. They were sluggish and reacting. Half were resting behind crenelations. "We can't hold them off much longer like this."

"What did you have in mind?" Ned stood straighter, and a smile actually came to his lips. Sam wasn't sure if it was hope or anticipation, but he returned the smile with one of his own.

"A surprise they won't forget."

Sam took Ned's place, a renewed strength flowing through his limbs. A ladder clunked on to the wall next to him. No one moved, so he gave them a glare and faced the man riding at the top of it.

"Are you willing to give up that easily? Are you not men of Chathem?" Sam swung the spear out and stabbed. The man on the ladder, clutching a sword in one hand, ducked.

Sam rapped his other hand on the knuckles with the flat of his spear. Instinctively the man let go and lost his footing at the same time.

He fell, clattering down into the fighters holding it. "You fear death, but death you will eat your fill of if they get a foothold here." Sam swung his spear around and pushed the ladder off with all his might. It fell, and he turned to face the others.

"You built this place," Sam said, swinging his spear around to point to a mason. "Your hands built this wall, a defense in troubled times for your future and that of your kin."

He pointed at another. "You set the crenelations, sweating to move them in place." He grabbed hold of Matthew, who was crouching down next to him. "You kept us safe and guarded these walls."

He had their attention now, and the fear was flowing from them. Now, something else replaced it. They were getting the will to fight back. "Are you willing to lay down your life in defense of your brother, your kin? Or will you let them take us and hang us from a pike for the birds to act?"

Grumblings now, and murmurers. It was starting to work. They were talking at least. "Rise to your feet, and fight."

The smell of smoke permeated the air, overriding all else. There was a respite in the attack as the Belmarchers gathered their strength.

Sam looked over the edge, hazarding a moment in the firing line. More dead and wounded than he expected.

One by one, the men along the wall rose. They got to their feet despite their wounds, their fears, and the enemy.

One by one, they rose to fight.

26

THE BEAR

"What are we supposed to do?" Matthew asked. Sam grabbed his hand and helped him to his feet. He almost slipped on the blood.

"Hold them off as long as you can. Make them pay for each foot they advance with arrow and rock." The Belmarchers were massing again, gathering the ladders for another attack. He ducked, narrowly avoiding another arrow. "Take out those archers."

The western wall was flagging again. Sam picked up a pole and handed it to a middle-aged mason. "Repel the ladders as long as you can."

Something caught his eye in the courtyard. Women, and the older children, were streaming out of the keep.

They had buckets, pans, pots, and even cups. Anything that could hold water.

Sam's heart soared. They could do this, they could repel this attack. They just had to hold on a little longer.

Men were coming over ladders, despite the defenders pushing them back. They were getting a foothold, and, with the distance he would have to run, Sam wasn't sure he could make it in time.

Then, he saw the largest man he had seen in his life. Over six feet tall, with a sword almost three feet long. His armor gleamed, and his eyes glowed.

The defenders fell back as he swung his sword, clearing a way for him to gain a foothold on the wall. Sam could almost smell the hate in his eyes, and his bloodlust. It radiated out like waves in a pond disturbed by a rock.

A brave guard attacked. The man knocked him away like he was a rag-doll, and he slammed into the stone.

Sam took off at a run, as fast as he dared across the uneven wall paving stones. He left the other attackers behind him to push off the ladders and blunt the advance.

The big man cleared out an area six feet wide, cutting through another defender, shoulder to hip. His sword stuck, and he kicked the body away. It tumbled into the courtyard and lay motionless, leaking blood.

This man had to be stopped, and at all costs. In a foreign tongue, he turned back to his men and urged them on, laughing at what could only have been an insult in his native language.

Despite the warmth of the sun Sam felt a chill run up his back. He had heard of men like this, and only had the misfortune of meeting one other in a fair fight.

And that was years ago, in his prime. Now, Sam was older and unpracticed.

But what was he to do? Turn and run? To where?

There was no running from this fight, not anymore.

A moment later and he was at the retreating flank of the defenders, then pushing through, yelling at them to move out of the way.

They had no problem letting him through, scrambling out of the way of the advancing Belmarchers.

Sam's eyes widened, and he drew up short. The man was even bigger up close.

"What have we here?" the man asked. Sam took a fighting stance, and breathed deep, leveling his spear.

Every second he delayed another attacker mounted the ladder. There were four of them over the edged, and a quick glance told him there were more coming.

In fact, the other attackers from the south were starting to round the corner, rushing on.

Sam returned his attention to the big man. There was nothing to say, so Sam stepped forward and attacked.

The tip of the spear shot forward, aimed at the throat.

The man batted it away without blinking an eye. The shock from the parry ran up the spear shaft and into Sam's hands.

It hurt.

He said something else in his language. The other attackers backed up and smiled. Sam crouched down and prepared for the assault.

His first attack may have been a feint, but the man was committed.

Huge, heavy swings of the sword parted the air. Sam had no time to parry them and ducked out of the way. He was fast for such a large man, too fast.

All Sam could do was move out of the way and retreat. Step by step they went south. Sam attempted a counterattack, but a mailed fist punched him in the face, sending him spinning.

Sam swallowed. His jaw felt like it had been pulled out of place.

He knew he was outmatched, and that there was only one likely outcome to this fight.

But there Trent was, still fighting. His leg was bleeding, and he had a cut over his left eye.

He dispatched an attacker with the help of a man from behind, then turned to ward off the ladders, grabbing hold of a pole and pushing.

Sam felt the sword coming and dropped, swinging at the same time and shooting his spear forward.

It caught the big man by surprise, and the spear buried deep into his thigh, slipping in between a plate and under leather.

There was surprise in his eyes, but Sam didn't hesitate. He wrenched his spear free and attacked.

His arms were waking up, remembering the forms he had worked so many times before. Thrust, pull, swing. Every opening he could exploit, he did.

Sam's advantage didn't last for long. With a grunt the big man tuned his spear and swung in a counterattack. Sam stepped back.

But not fast enough.

The sword cut through his shoulder. The smell of iron filled the air. The adrenaline overrode the pain, but Sam knew he would feel it.

the big man smiled at him. "Too weak. You're all too weak."

Sam panted, each lung a painful lance. "We kept you out this long."

"Your time for life is over." The big man's smile turned into a snarl.

His attacks came faster, and somehow stronger. Sam fell back again. He was losing ground too quickly, there wouldn't be enough wall left.

Then Sam felt the hard south wall behind him and knew he had run out of time.

27

Against Rock

Sam was at the south end of the wall. The big man thrust, nearly skewering him. Without room to maneuver, fear choked him.

He was breathing hard, harder than he had in his life, but his body knew what to do. Sam cleared his mind, letting it take over.

There was nothing left but to let go. He would either die here, or he would die later.

"Now is the time of your death, little one." The man cleft the air just above his head, and Sam struck him on the right knee. He pulled back his sword across Sam's right shoulder, slicing through skin to the bone.

He cried out, then ducked out of the way of another attack, turning onto the south wall. A northern wind was blowing, the sun beginning its descent in the western sky.

The big man squinted, and Sam saw his chance. "Over here you big oaf." Blood pouring down his arm, he dragged his spear across the rock and retreated a few steps.

Other defenders had retreated with him, unwilling or unable to help the fight. Sam didn't blame them, but he didn't have time to keep track of them.

The big man turned and roared, squinting and swinging wildly. It was easier to dodge, the weight of his armor finally having an effect.

Sam slipped past his attack, light and free of plate mail. Seeing his advantage return rejuvenated him, energy flowing back to his limbs despite his aches and pains.

Sam got closer, trading a few punches to the head and receiving one in return that sent him flying back and seeing stars.

He caught his backward movement, jaw aching, and had to immediately parry a thrust to the side. It caught his abdomen, cutting through him on the left.

Now, losing blood and feeling the pain through the adrenaline, he set his stance.

The big man was laughing, an unpleasant, grating sound that filled him with dread. His sword came in from the left.

Sam caught it with the tip of his spear, spinning it down and smashing the butt of his spear alongside the big man's head.

It snapped over, and he stepped back.

The man smiled again, spat out a few teeth, and was back on the attack.

They traded blows. Sam was flagging, unable to keep up with the sheer strength of the man. He was like a wild animal that, no matter how many wounds it had, refused to die.

Sam stumbled, the rock under his left side giving way, and scrambled back to safety. He got another cut for the distraction across his chest.

He is toying with me.

Sam panted, heart racing faster than a horse in gallop. Blood soaked his right arm, and he had to tighten his grip on his spear.

The sun was in his eyes again, but Sam knew that would be no help.

Evan winced, hearing the scream cut short. Was that one of his subjects or the enemy? His hands trembled around the cup, splashing wine to the floor in drips.

He couldn't help but notice they looked like big stains of blood.

He should be out there, fighting alongside Yand and the others, but here he was, cowering like a coward.

His sword lay across his desk, his armor donned, and his uniform immaculate. The same could not be said for those outside.

Duke Hornblood stared up at the crest above his desk. He was a Hornblood, and the Duke. He would rule his father's lands someday when he was gone.

So why couldn't he go and fight for them?

Yand had known his character all along, despite his years of teachings and urging. That look on his face as he left.

It stung the young Duke.

He slammed down his wine, angry at himself and the world. He didn't ask for these circumstances, didn't ask for glory.

And he didn't ask to be thrust into battle with no army to support him.

His father would have levied his forces had he known, come marching north to beat back the Belmarch and put them in his place.

Eyes cast to the side, he hung his head and shuffled back to the wine bottle, pouring the last few drops into his glass.

He drank them, then retreated to his chair. He wanted to shut up his ears, to ignore the cries and screams, the clashes. He wanted to ignore the smells, horrible smells that came into his room. Blood and fire, bile and waste.

A knock summoned him from his wine induced stupor. Even that couldn't give him courage.

"Leave me in peace."

"Sire, it is Captain Yand." *Here to give me a tongue lashing, no doubt to urge me into the fight.*

"Tell him to get me when he's won." There was a pause, then whispers.

This wasn't right. Yand should have been pounding at the door himself.

So why hadn't he?

Like a lapdog, he was forced to follow the young Duke around, to be a protector and guide. To satisfy his mother and her suffocating ways.

He had found him in the streets, dressed as a commoner and passed out in the gutter, dusted him off and brought him back.

Not once had he gone to his father with a bad report to bring him under his wrath. No, Yand had done that all himself, with those disappointed looks and refusals to chastise.

Rousing himself, Duke Hornblood stumbled across the room and wrenched open the door.

Two servants, shocked at seeing him, mouths opened, stood before him. In anger, he opened his mouth.

Then, he saw Yand.

"No. No, it cannot be." The Duke took one step back as the servants recovered their composure and shock turned to fear.

"There was no saving him," one said, voice trembling.

Duke Evan Hornblood staggered against the door frame and slipped to his knees.

Captain Yand was dead.

All was lost.

28

OVERTURNING

Trent yanked out the sword and kicked, sending the man flying back down the ladder. It never seemed to help, they kept coming no matter what they did.

"Push." Trent and another man used the pole to tip the ladder back, hands below grabbing it to keep it on the wall.

They managed to push it far enough back it tipped over, but just like before, the attackers picked it back up, repositioning it and tilting it back into place.

He was tired, exhausted. He wanted to sit down and rest, to stop his cuts from bleeding.

But there was no time for that.

Men yelled beside him, urging them to keep it away. Like a beam in place, the ladder snapped in between the crenelations.

Trent took up a pole someone had dropped and set it against the ladder. he pushed.

And slipped.

The pole went between rungs, and he grabbed a hold of it and he leaned left, then toppled over.

The pole caught the side of the ladder, stopping his fall. It shook as a man started climbing.

It moved. It seemed like the ladders always stayed together, lashed by thick ropes too strong to simply cut away. They were resilient, made to stay together.

What was it that Sam had said? There's a way to break anything, given the right leverage.

It had to be thirty feet tall, made from thick trunks split in quarters. The rungs gave it stability, but it was the sides that kept it together.

"Help me," Trent said to the nearest defender, back turned to him. "We need to break these ladders, and I have an idea."

The man turned, and all the blood drained from Trent's face.

It was Bill.

But there was no time to be afraid now, not in the thick of battle. A vicious-looking man was three quarters of the way up.

"Twist it, make it fall over this way." Trent motioned with the wall, then made sure the pole was set.

Bill was covered in blood, but didn't seem to have a scratch on him. Trent didn't stop to think of why. He only hesitated a second, then set down his sword, taken from an attacker, then grabbed onto the pole.

Together, they pulled. The ladder scraped against the wall, but hands at the bottom held it up. It was heavy and took all the strength they had to move.

The ladder twisted, then popped out over the crenelation. "Next one," Trent said, gasping between words. Sweat poured down his head.

They took the pole out and moved it, leveraging again. The ladder resisted at first, but it gave way again.

"One more," Bill said, panting. They moved to the next one.

The ladder creaked and groaned, the attacker almost at eye level. They were out of arrows now. No way to get him off but by pushing or hand to hand combat.

Trent pushed with all his might. The ladder moved, crept over. The attacker took another step, sword in hand and eyes flashing.

That was all it took.

His weight shifting caught, then the ladder screeched against the wall as it started to fall.

One side caught a crenelation, then twisted and snapped. The ladder landed on its side, broken in two.

Others had seen it, and a great cheer went up. They copied the tactic, defenders tipping the ladders over and sending them cracking and crashing to the side.

Within a few minutes the wall was clear, the attackers frustrated and yelling on the ground below.

"Give them what they really want, boy," Bill said, picking up a chuck of rock and tossing it in the air. He threw it down with two hands, hitting the leg of a man with a sickening crack.

Trent slumped against the side of the wall, letting his body recover. The sun warmed his skin. A fresh breeze cooled his sweat soaked hair and brought with it the smell of the river, fresh and light above all the stench of fighting.

The guardhouse was burning, or it looked that way. A long line of women and children passed buckets and pots of water down a line up to it.

The vessels went in full and came out empty. Trent wasn't sure where it all was going, but as he looked closer, he realized it wasn't the gatehouse that was on fire, but something below the gatehouse.

The gate.

The thought passed through him like a ghost, chilling him to the bone. It was still holding, but orange dancing flames were visible through the hole in the middle, made by something large.

Then movement took his gaze to the south wall.

It was Sam.

He was fighting the largest man Trent had ever seen, and it looked like he was losing. The big man's sword knocked away his spear like a sliver.

Trent leaned down and picked up the strange sword. It was slick with blood, still warm but cool to his touch.

Only the east and west were in jeopardy now. Attackers trickled in, fighting to keep their foothold from defenders to the north and on the stairs up.

The guards at the southern wall were stuck behind Sam, unable to do anything but watch and fall back as he did.

"Bill, look." Bill swung his head around, seeing the problem in an instant.

"To the east," Bill said, flicking the blood from the tip of his sword and starting down the stairs.

Trent went with him, anxiously glancing up at Sam. The bear of a man hammered at him, over and over again.

His sword flashed in the evening light, wickedly swinging and drawing more and more blood.

Sam's clothes were in tatters. Trent had to do something.

His eyes played across the wall, looking for something, anything.

What could he do?

Archie and Ned were there, still shooting arrows at the attackers below.

"Ned," Trent said. He kept shooting, the closest to Sam. Trent gathered his breath, then screamed at the top of his lungs. "Ned!"

29

DEATHRATTLE

A hand shot out, wrapping around the shaft of his spear. Sam ducked the sword, pulling to try and free his weapon.

But the big man held fast. He gave a yank. Sam tumbled forward.

The man reeked. Not only of death, but of a foul odor from those that wallow in filth.

Sam twisted, trying to get out of his grip. The big man squeezed him tight, crushing him.

There was no air in his lungs. The armor poked into him, an unyielding mass that threatened to break his bones.

The world started going dark. Sam tried to breathe, fought for air. He didn't know when it had happened, but there was a hand around his throat.

I'm going to die.

It was all he could think. He tried to picture his sister, his mother. Someone.

But he couldn't. Thoughts had fled. The darkness closed in.

Then he was gasping for air at the man's feet as he laughed above him.

Sam struggled to his feet. The man punched him. "Put up a decent fight. Not great. I'll enjoy killing you."

Sam couldn't respond. He was still trying to catch his breath.

The big man snapped his spear in two with one hand. It parted like a reed bent by the wind.

The two halves fell to the floor of the wall, and he kicked the spear head off. It clattered on the way down, too far out of reach.

It landed point down in the dirt below.

Metal rasped on rock. Sparks flew, drawing Sam's attention back.

The big man was not smiling now.

His sword was scratching down the wall. It was clear what he intended to do with it.

"Ned!" Trent's voice rang out clear and loud, above all the other sounds.

He was running across the courtyard, a sword in hand.

He had viewed Sam as a coward, watched him refuse to fight.

Now, in his last hour, would he let him see the same again?

The broken spear shaft was between them, right at his feet. Sam searched every inch of him and saw only one place it would do any good on the big man.

He just needed an opening, he just needed some time.

Sam tensed up, prepared to move.

The man raised his sword high above his head. Sam knew he would swing through and would drop to the right.

That might be enough.

Then, an arrow blossomed on the big man's hand. The sword clattered to the ground.

Sam dove, grabbing what was left of the spear shaft just as the man turned in a fury that dwarfed all others.

There was more than murder in his eyes. This man would not stop at Sam, he would continue to the others.

Then the women, then the children.

Sam plunged the jagged, splintered end right into his eye.

There was a briefest hesitation of resistance, then it squelched in.

Bile rising in his throat, Sam pushed as hard as he could, ignoring the scream that chilled him to the bone and touched his very soul.

It crunched deeper, then home.

The scream stopped, and the man fell on him.

Together they tumbled, and Sam hit his head against the wall.

Light. Voices. A tunnel. He wanted to stay asleep. It was so comfortable.

Then, a touch.

Where am I?

Sounds, like someone talking through water.

The light faded. The sounds cleared. Hands pulled at him.

Sam was on his feet. His hands wouldn't move. But that wasn't right.

They did. He tested them.

" — done it. You've shown them. They're running like dogs now!" Matthew was triumphant, pounding him on the back.

He shook his head, regained his senses.

The attackers were being driven back and retreating in full.

The big man had been the one driving them on. And now he lay face down on the wall, propped up by the spear that projected from his head.

"Is he?" Sam asked, mouth full of what felt like cotton.

"Dead. Like a rock." The defenders made quick work of the two attackers who remained, overwhelming them within seconds.

Sam's legs trembled. They felt like jelly. The smell of smoke. The guardhouse. The gate!

Children and women were passing water to it, and now the men joined in.

They threw the water down the murder holes, dousing the flames. The attackers were retreating now, fleeing across the field.

Sam looked at them, leaderless and confused.

Now would be the perfect time for a counterattack.

To ride out and run them down, ending the siege once and for all.

But he had no army.

"To the gate," Sam said. He stepped forward, then almost fell.

"No, you don't. You'll rest here, with me." Sam looked up, Ned's smiling, old weathered face looking up at him.

"Was that...?"

"Yes. I can put my mark where I need it, given the right amount of prodding." Ned jerked his head over to the courtyard. "You wouldn't be alive if it wasn't for him."

Trent was leading the others at the well. He was passing out water, dunking the bucket as fast as he could and pouring it into the waiting containers.

Sam embraced him, partially supporting himself on the old man. "I wouldn't be alive if it wasn't for you."

"We aren't safe yet." Sam released the embrace, and Ned followed his gaze. He sat down on the wall, leaning up against the crenelation.

"You don't think they'll leave?"

"No. They fought like animals to kill us. Predators that persistent won't let us go." The smoke was lessening now, the water having its intended effect.

The sun was setting, casting a golden hue on the world. The sky was soft red, unlike the harsh color of blood, and yellow and orange.

The wind was blowing away the smoke, and the accompanying smell. It turned black, then white, then faded as Sam watched the enemy retreat to their encampment.

"We've done it. We've beat them." Ned stood beside Sam, making sure h didn't fall.

Sam closed his eyes and rested.

They'd beat them, for now.

The castle was quiet now, the still of night descending like a blanket. Only the vultures talked, breaking the night's stillness with their quarrels and fights.

There were so many dead, and many more wounded. Archie was found in the courtyard, and his wife refused to leave his side.

She cried bitter tears and cursed the castle for taking her husband.

Sam cried with her. For the man that Archie was and could have been.

His body joined a long line that started with one, then two, then grew to fourteen.

And Captain Yand among them.

Duke Hornblood had come out of his room, briefly, to look after the men. He had turned and fled back into his room when they started moving in the bodies.

Sam helped, muscles aching and body torn, or tried to. He had to stop often and catch his breath, bandages covering his body.

"You need to go lie down and rest," Martha said.

"I'll rest when the work is finished." Sam knew there was a long road ahead, and more tears and sadness.

Trent came up to him after they were done, each man covered in a blanket to hide his face from the world, for they would never look upon it again.

"Thank you," Sam said.

"I didn't do anything you didn't teach me." Trent was blushing, barely visible in the torchlight.

"You reminded me that I might not be able to pick the battles I fight." A young carpenter, holding his own against hardened fighters.

Trent was going to do fine.

He shifted. "Sam?"

"Yes?"

"How are we..."

The moon sat among the stars, plump and white.

"We'll find a way."

Excerpt from Winter at Hornblood Castle: Epic of Hornblood Castle #2

"Still there?" Ned joined Sam on the wall, staring out over the bloodstained field. Winter was around the corner, the winds turning cold and biting when the sun went down. Leaves were falling now, most of the gold, brown, and red coating the forest floor.

"Still there." Sam pulled at his coat, itching his bandages. A few days hadn't done much to heal them. "Shouldn't you be asleep?"

"I should be asking you the same question." Ned's beard and mustache had grown out, just as bushy, if not more so, than his eyebrows. They couldn't hide the gauntness of his cheeks, though.

"Give me a few minutes, I'll be in. Any word from Overseer Rhys?" There was another question to that, deeper.

"That's your realm, not mine."

Captain Yand had left a deep hole, one that Sam hoped the young Duke would fill. So far, though...

"He's young, give him time." *Not that young.* Twenty was more than old enough to be a journeyman apprentice, if not a full carpenter.

The thought reminded him of Archie. His gaze was pulled over to the freshly mounded sections of earth in the corner of the castle. That, Overseer Rhys had done well to execute. The ceremony had been short, the mourners few, but the entire castle had been there. Duke Hornblood included.

Forty-seven. Forty-seven men remained alive within the walls to man and fight. Another thirty-five women and children on top of that.

A heron skimmed along the tree line, then dipped into the river beyond. It was far outside of their line of sight now.

"I'll go inside." Sam stood up, aches and pains twitching at him. Ned clapped him on the shoulder, which brought a sting with it.

"Sorry. Get some rest."

The fires of the Belmarch burned well beyond the arrow range of their bows. Sam had hoped they would give up without a leader, that they would slink back across the river in the dead of the night one day. That hadn't happened. Now, he doubted it ever would.

They had burned their dead on pyres, the bodies that they could. Sam had ordered the others dumped into the river. The pillars that had gone up then were big, and white. The fires burned hot, consumed everything, including flesh and bone. *Whatever they believed, their dead were gone, just like ours.*

Sam limped down the stairs, feeling a pang in his left foot every time he set it down, but eventually made it to the bottom. He went back into the Keep, only to find Bill leaning against the wall, waiting for him.

"Sam," Bill said. Sam was startled by the interruption and almost dropped the door on himself.

"Yes?"

"May we... talk?"

Sam nodded, and Bill went back out with him, back across the yard and into his stone hut. The room was cool, warmer than the outside air, but not by much. Bill offered a chair and

Sam took it, sighing as the weight came off his left foot. The small fireplace tucked into one wall was barren and dusty. A spiderweb was strung along one corner. Even Bill couldn't escape the lack of fuel and wood, a prudent rule set by the Overseer. With winter coming, though...

"We need to break free of this siege," Bill said.

"We're in agreement." A long silence stretched between them. Sam was wary. He didn't trust Bill yet. "What do you propose?"

"Kill them all." Bill shrugged. "They won't leave on their own."

The shack smelled of mildew. The floor was damp somehow, even though they hadn't had rain in a while, near the fireplace. Sam shifted in the chair to get more comfortable, easing the way it was digging into his back.

"Easier said than done." His voice was full of sarcasm.

"You know the Duke isn't cut out for this." Bill shook his head. "I don't know where he's been hiding his stash of booze, but I'd love to know where." He licked his lips. "Loves it more than I ever did."

Sam looked into his eyes, the strange look of truthfulness in them. *Was that true, or was it just what he believed?*

"We can't force him to act."

"We have to." Bill pointed out his window. "Or do you want to die here? They'll tear us limb from limb and feed us to the dogs if they could."

He jabbed at the large bandages wrapped around his torso. "Or did you forget the man who gave you that?"

Sam frowned. Mention of it made his wound burn and itch. It hurt, but only grazed his ribcage. "I remember."

"He would have broken you earlier, had he not wanted to toy with you, make you an example."

"He's dead now," Sam reminded him.

"But another will rise in his place."

"How do you know so much about the Belmarch?" Sam squinted at him, examining his face, his hands.

"I've lived near the border all my life. It's impossible not to know them." Bill leaned in closer. "If you did, you'd hate them like I do."

Sam didn't see where this was going, and the look in Bill's eyes made him uncomfortable. The man was small and wiry, but somehow he had managed to escape the fight with a few cuts and scratches. And Trent said he was covered in blood. How he managed to do that, Sam had a burning desire to know, but at the same time didn't.

"We can agree on all of this," Sam sat back. "So, what does it have to do with me?" He crossed his arms.

"You're a fighting man, but not just any fighting man." Bill leaned in more. "You could take control, lead us out of this place."

"That sounds an awful lot like a revolt."

"Revolt? No. Such a strong word. Such a dirty word." Bill held up his hands, as if innocent. "You're not just a fighter, are you?"

"I've seen my share of bloodshed. I want to put it behind me, to leave it where it belongs. No man should kill another."

"Come now, Sam. We both know better. Men must die, either by another man's hands or of old age. Why is it that certain men keep the privilege for themselves?"

"Is that what the Belmarch think? That any man can kill another?" There was something wrong in the words. Twisted, perverted. They made so much sense, but didn't feel right.

A child yelled in the courtyard. It made Sam stop, but the sound of laughter followed, and he relaxed.

"I want to survive just as badly as any other man, but there are some things I'll not do."

Bill's eyes watched him, dark and foreboding. "We'll see how well you keep that word."

Sam stood up, unable to be in the man's presence anymore. "I take my leave of you." His voice was gruff and short. Bill nodded but said nothing.

An unpleasant man. Always had been, always will be. Sam was glad to shut the door behind him, even though the day had faded into twilight and brought with it more chill.

How long had it been? A few months? A few weeks? Weariness overtook him, burrowing deep into his bones. Everything seemed to blend together. He went to bed troubled, not seeing a way forward, no path of survival.

"How do you propose we do that?" Evan took another sip. He turned the goblet in his hand, examining it in the failing light. It was dirty, smudged with fingerprints, and streaked. That was what he could see, in better light he suspected it would be worse. It smelled better than it looked, the aroma of the dark, red wine pleasantly floral. Better than the smell of death and blood, or the commoners that stunk.

"I still have some pull in the capital." Overseer Rhys sat across from him. "Provided I can get to them, there are those who would still listen to me."

He was fat, but not as much as he used to be. Evan's stomach grumbled, but he ignored it. Wine would help with that, too.

"Do you have an army that can sally forth and break a hole in the invader's ranks? Or perhaps a secret passage you've been hiding from me that goes straight to the King's chambers?" Duke Evan rubbed his eyes. He wearied of this topic, which had come up more frequently since...He was gone.

Through the buzz in his head, he knew that. He wished he were still here now, standing beside him with that disappointed look.

"No..." The Overseer shifted in his seat.

"Then let us speak of it no more." He was tired and lonely. Even the Overseer was too far below his rank to be called a friend in this place. Even a cousin would be better than nothing. He'd even take Theo, brash and stupid as he was, for a companion than rot away here.

The Overseer clearly wanted to talk more of it, but he cleared his throat and took out a scrap of parchment. "Shall we proceed to inventory, then?"

Evan cringed. "Go on."

"Barrels of flour, thirty-two. Barrels of biscuit, fifteen. Boxes of nails, ten. Quarried stone, fifteen thousand pieces..." The Overseer went down his list, order unchanged from last time. Food continued to decrease, as did everything else.

He droned on. Evan drank more, then emptied his goblet. He thought about filling it up, but the long list was making him sleepy.

Then something caught his attention.

"Casks of wine, three. Bottles of wine, seventeen."

Evan sat up. "Stop. What was that?"

The Overseer licked his lips, wrinkled his brow, and went over his list again. "Oak, seven stacks?"

"The wine."

"Ah. Three casks, seventeen bottles."

"I thought we had over twenty bottles last week." His heart palpitated. It didn't sound bad until he thought back to the first inventory. Double the casks and over a hundred bottles of his own personal stock had accompanied him here.

The Overseer's mouth was working, but no sound came out.

"Answer me," he said.

"We did, sire."

"Then who took it?" Another long pause.

"Wine has only been issued to your Highness."

"What? No." He ran through the week in his head. There was no way he had drunk that much wine. Or was there?

His head buzzed, and he stood up and went to the bar with the bottle. It was almost empty. He opened the case up with his key. A quick count confirmed it, then another count. Seventeen bottles, standing like sentinels.

"It can't be. Someone has been stealing from me."

"Sire—"

"I don't want excuses, Rhys, I want answers. Find the man that did this and bring him to me." He drained the bottle into his goblet. Half a glass, at best. It tasted sickly sweet.

"I will conduct an investigation," the Overseer's eyes drooped. "And I will report all that I can find."

"Good. Carry on." The wine went to his head, made him feel drowsy. The long list of supplies didn't help. He wasn't paying attention, even long after the Overseer had concluded and tucked away his paper. He was thinking about his father and uncle. What would they do if they were in his situation? Would they ride out, breastplate burnished and gleaming, to lead a fatal charge and break the enemy line? Or would they do what he was doing, hide away here in the safety of his walls and wait for the inevitable to happen?

He cursed his luck, and his own stupidity for pushing his father to send him, and for Yand for not stopping him.

Even through the fog of the wine he knew that wasn't quite right. The memory of that night came back, the low conversation, Yand imploring him to wait until the castle was finished. But he had pushed for this, to distinguish himself and prove his mettle.

He stared into the goblet. Was this all he could do? Was this his character?

The Overseer stared at him. Evan realized he had been calling his name for some time.

"Yes?"

"What are your orders, sire?"

His orders? His orders? A spark of anger tried to ignite, but it found nothing inside him to burn. Instead, it smoldered. Evan looked upon Rhys with contempt. What right did he have to demand from Duke Hornblood?

"I grow tired." His speech was starting to slur. "Leave me."

The Overseer clamped his mouth shut and stood. He gathered his robes. "Goodnight, your Highness."

He left. Evan stood in front of his desk, staring up at the crest of his family as tears rolled down his cheek.

Get Winter at Hornblood

Eclectic Stories

Thank you for spending your precious time reading this book.

If stories make you salivate, learn more about lore, take an exclusive sneak peek behind the scenes, and get writing updates in my newsletter, Eric's Eclectic Stories.

As a bonus you'll get *Stories from the Deep*, a Patmos Sea Fantasy Adventure anthology that gives a glimpses of lore, extra prologues and epilogues, and character backstories.

If you aren't satisfied, unsubscribe at any time.

Join at erickercher.com.

-Eric Kercher

ALSO BY ERIC KERCHER

Patmos Sea Fantasy Adventure Series

*Fathomless Pursuit - Architect's Prize - Ironbound Path
Sunken Prey – Unanswered Prophecy – Hardened Pilgrim –
Final Peace*

Seventh Hall Chronicles

Seventh Hall - Ode to the Survivors - Bastion of the Deep

Epic of Hornblood Castle

*Siege of the Unfinished Keep – Winter at Hornblood – Branch
of the Everlong*

Castlebound Adventures

Rats in the Cellar!- Save the Cat!

ERIC KERCHER

Collections

Red Eagle Anthology – Searchlight Anthology

Stand Alone

Planet Reaping – Dukedom Rumble – Savage Space Salvage

About Author

Eric Kercher was born and raised in a small town on the Great Plains on good books. After attending a small state school on the east coast he joined the US Navy to serve his country and explore the world. He worked on submarines, and the world beneath the waves captivated him with all its mysteries and wonders. After spending time in larger cities, he's settled down in a quiet town with his wife and children. When not on an adventure in a good book the author enjoys creating dust woodworking, architecture, and spending time with loved ones.

Find out more at www.erickercher.com.

* 9 7 8 1 9 6 5 8 7 1 0 0 3 *